Creedmore Fleenor

In passing through

Creedmore Fleenor

In passing through

ISBN/EAN: 9783337254728

Printed in Europe, USA, Canada, Australia, Japan

Cover: Foto ©Andreas Hilbeck / pixelio.de

More available books at **www.hansebooks.com**

CREEDMORE FLEENOR.

———o———

AUTHOR'S EDITION.   LIMITED.

———o———

BOWLING GREEN, KY.
Courier Pub. Co.,
1898.

IN PASSING THROUGH!

I.

A change is come, selah! The scold
  Of bitter days we bid farewell;
The biting winds are not so bold;
The frost has left the ground and cold
  Is nothing that earth's warmth can swell.

She basks within the sun's bright rays
  And nurtures all within her bourne,
She fondles, in capricious ways,
The offspring of her waxing days,
  And quirks and jollies each in turn.

Old Winter's mantle that still clings,
  She shakes from shoulders glowing fair;
With prodigality she flings
The seed of everything that springs,
  And tends each with a mother's care.

She ushers into life each bud
  That promises a blooming prime;
She gives them drink within the flood—
Her rushing torrent is the blood
  That courses in the veins of Time.

II.

The daring crocus through the snow
    Doth raise his head; the buttercup,
And violet of modest glow,
And dandelion, too, would show
    Their hardihood in struggling up

To brave inclemencies and prove
    The glory of their being here,
Which renders brilliant field and grove,
And makes the world a thing to love
    With all its beauties blushing near.

And grass and herb and shrubby tree,
    In many colored liveries,
Bud out to blend the sky and lea
In rainbow tints; and busy bee
    Hums merrily upon the breeze.

The early rose with bursting bloom,
    And May-bells that the fairies ring,
Now serve to dissipate the gloom
The winter knew and start the loom
    Of Life aweaving in the spring.

III.

Hail to the Spring! Fair infant year
    That wails and sobs as any child!
That shrieks with laughter till a tear
Steals from the frown that darkens cheer—
    Now tempest-tost, now blandly mild!

Thou art the season of sweet youth;
   The Ragnarok of Essence sped:
And Life that felt the winter's ruth,
New blooms again to bless the truth
   That Nature slept and was not dead:

Thy pallor blushes rosy hue,
   Thy silence breaks into a song,
And hoary frost and clammy dew,
Warm into babbling brooks anew
   To dance and birl and vault along.

And clothed in verdure is the scene
   That late was grim and stark in death,
While lowering clouds, which hung between
The azure sky and earth, are seen
   In fragments tost by Summer's breath.

We drink thy charms within the wind
   That blows the buds of vernal bloom;
We greet thy beauties unconfined,
Thy fragrance steals within the mind
   That winter numbed with all its gloom.

IV.

O fickle Day of smiles and tears,
   We laugh and weep thy humors too!
In youth we chatter with our fears
And trust each phantom that appears;
   In age we find the hour's rue!

How like thy tempests to this Soul
  That sinks or swells with every throb;
How like thy elements' control
That through vicissitudes would roll
  To burst into a smile, a sob!

How like all earthly things we see
  That feel the pulse of Time and Tide;
How like the soul unto the sea,
The trembling main to man when he
  Doth feel the shock of rage and pride:

And yet these Sentiencies, unlike
  The duller molecules of clay,
Pass off the stage of life, and dike
Is earth for that which seemeth like,
  And Youth is born but to decay!

Could life forever be as thou,
  So full of pleasure and of cheer,
Man would no thought of grief allow,
For every fancy would prove how
  Love's pleasures brood from year to year.

V.

For Childhood, in thy morn's delight,
  Thy thoughts do revel in sweet dreams;
Fair visions float before thy sight,
Thy powers feel a doughty might
  To stem the rush of Stygian streams:

All space is peopled by thy guile,
   And fancy lives and joy bestows,
And Love is cooing all the while,
And everywhere a happy smile
   Tells of the heart that overflows :

Through haze the world in grandeur floats
   With beauties full in its display,
And, like the miser's soul that gloats
O'er riches, thou to richer notes
   Give sway to bless each happy day :

Thou livest in the checkered shade,
   With bird and bee and wilder flower,
Where some fair Amaryllis played,
Or Daphnis with his shyer maid —
   Sweet Chloris, of the woodland bower.

In amplitude of youth thy hope
   Is king of life and its reward ;
Thy nascent wisdom sees the scope
Of wish alone ; thy joy doth ope
   The heart to every sounding chord.

VI.

O Day of Youth and Love ! O Spring !
   O Tide of human guile ! O Thought
That comes with all and gives us wing
To soar aloft, a voice to sing
   The anthems of the heart : for aught

We know thou art some Sentiency
    Eternal as the earth or sky;
A spirit that doth come to free
The duller Soul and Latency
    Bound here by some nefaric tie!

But whether Spirit, Time or Tide
    That animates or ebbs or flows,
Thou art, O Spring, a season's pride,
A flux of joys with boundaries wide,
    A day when simple Nature glows.

Thou art the season of sweet love:
    For truly is it said of thee,
Thy day doth mark the mating dove,
Thy flood the swelling of each love
    Here glowing for its company:

For thou art Eros of the lore
    Delightful to the Grecian ear,
The Cupid that has gone before
To leave Love's courtship in the glow
    Of romance, lingering year to year:

The Force that binds its power's might
    In taming hearts too fierce or wild;
That brings within the soul the light
Which casts its radiance to the night,
    That fills the heart of winter's child:

Fair season of the passion's glow,
  Rejuvenation speaks welcome;
And all the roses thou canst blow,
Fling out and let old Winter know
  That Age is dead and Youth is come!

VII.

For passions of the heart but stir
  To prove that all the world is kin,
And that each soul's existence here
Depends on love, and every care
  Arises from the strife to win

A happy home, a love, a life,
  A sounding fame, a hope, a name,
A blissful peace, a joy, a wife,
A fierce contest with worldly strife,
  And glory in each passion's flame;

And in pursuit we find the chase
  Alluring to the sense and mind;
We so forget ourselves and place
The guerdon far above the race
  That leaves us feeble in its wind.

When Spring brings love to every heart,
  And opens flood-gates of the soul,
How cold were Life to know no part
Of love, nor feel the burning dart
  Which amorous dreams would here control.

Phlegmatic is old Death; its chill
  The absence of deific fire:
The pulse of Life is passion's thrill;
The ichor of its god is still
  The blood and flood of Youth's desire.

In courtship days how fair the sky,
  How bright the world, how sweet the lays
Of cooing birds that carol high
In leafy bowers, and reply
  In chirps of happy answering praise!

How sweet the flowers, and the breeze
  Is warm with sensual breath of love;
And happy laughter tells of ease,
And sun-rays flit among the trees
  Like elfins in a fairy cove:

And so idylic is the dream
  Of Youth with sunny thoughts of peace:
And burning love is what 'twould seem,
And heart and soul with visions teem —
  Drunk with their own wild love's increase.

Sing out, bright Love, and let the heart
  Rejoice in its youth and spring!
The soul is happy though thy part
Is mingled with some passing smart
  That leaves a tittle of its sting.

The sweet remains to cheer the day
  When love is fled or is no more ;
For dream will ever covet lay
Which once awoke a joyous day
  That held a love within its glow :

And, fleeting though the hour be,
  Much good attends thy passing state ;
For cherished in rich memory
Are scenes which live forever free
  Of that to cloy or satiate :

And thoughts are always young, 'tis said,
  Though brow is wrinkled, hair is gray,
And virile nimbleness is fled
To join the seasons that are sped
  From chill December back to May.

X.

Thy humor, Spring, is lot of all ;
  Thy love-tide moves each sensuous will ;
' Tis not with man alone thy call,
But rapture would each heart enthrall
  And teach each voice an amorous trill :

And here within the slumberous shades.
  As on the new spring swath I lie,
I hear the chirpings in the glades,
Frogs croaking their bass serenades
  To silent loves that hover nigh ;

And elytrons the crickets thrum —
 Harps of the voiceless things of life!
And in the brooks the fishes drum,
And all the earth seems roused to hum
 Of lowly creatures in love's strife :

And birds within the tree-tops high,
 Are trilling sweetest melody,
And, with their loves, so coy and shy,
I drink the flood of song and sigh
 For notes of such wild harmony!

If man could sing like these his sphere
 Were one of bliss however low ;
For each sweet note would rouse and stir
The soul of rapture, and the cheer
 Were all his being here would know.

He would not feel his narrow bounds,
 Nor note the hobble of his gait ;
But, borne aloft on quivering sounds,
His soul were free of lowly bounds
 And saltant in the blissful state!

XI.

Sing. birds!   Within ethereal realms
 Our mundane troubles know ye not!
Ye can not be disturbed with dreams
Which horror man, for joy seems
 The measure of your happy lot.

Above the earth and all its rue
  That hangs an incubus to me,
Ye float and sing as if ye knew
No earthly pain; your azure blue
  Were all divine and full of glee!

'Tis boastful man with god-like mind,
  That fate has fettered to the earth :
Ye choristers of the sky, on wind
Can drift and be so unconfined
  Ye scorn the things of lowly birth!

At morn some praise to Deity
  Awakes the matins of your song;
Ye soar aloft with gladsome cry —
I, here below. heave answering sigh,
  And watch the earth's poor, madd'ning throng!

At night your voice is lullaby
  To rankling tumult of the day,
And sweet nocturnes of melody
Teach wakeful souls some harmony,
  And lull the troubled thoughts away :

Away from strife and toil which left
  Their stings to fester unto death;
Which filled the souls of men bereft
Of hope or faith — which only left
  A way for your sweet chanting breath!

VII.

The unsubstantial is the lure
　Of souls aspiring things most high;
We live in dreams and deem as sure
The vagueness of our thoughts; and pure
　Each heart and soul by its own sigh.

And so we pass our idle times
　And live in realms to us unknown;
See pleasure worlds and tropic climes;
Hear choral notes of heaven's chimes;
　Build airy castles all our own!

We clothe the lands in rainbow hues,
　We note the smiling skies in seas;
And virgin nature we would choose
For Romance to regale its views
　And catch the languor of the breeze.

Could we forever live as when
　The Golden Age blessed all mankind,
Our earthly home and Eden then
Were sure, and we in viny glen
　Might romp in freedom unconfined.

But we through sterner duty move
　And load ourselves with vain concerns,
And labor only here to prove
The falacy of every move
　We make in following human turns.

It matters not were born or how,
  Or whether love bespoke our birth,
The seasons move; the times allow
Brief respite to a youthful vow:
  Prone are the children of this earth!

A burden each must bear, forsooth,
  Though lame and hobble be his gait;
And howsoever blank his youth,
Or irksome be the weight of ruth,
  He must still onward to his fate.

He must still onward though his dreams
  Fade into vacancy and night;
He must not loll in Fancy's beams,
Nor eddy on the sluggish streams
  Where Romance loiters in delight.

XIII.

Before us soon two roads stretch out —
  The one to honor and to fame,
The other mediocre route
Where fortune is the idle bout
  Of spirits that are weak and tame.

Which road now take who best can say,
  Since pilgrims journeying are at odds?
Each would advise the other way;
Each would recount the bitter pay
  Rewarding manhood's lagging plods.

We stand and list to passing sighs —
  To choose the one of loudest boast!
Unlike the Hero whose surmise
Was that each labor brought its prize
  And nothing came without its cost.

We move but blindly and we find
  A disappointment in the end;
We turn aside from evil kind,
But in some other ill we bind
  The error we had thought to mend.

XIV.

Ambitions tempt us all.   We think
  Great ends are for us to achieve,
And vast our power to do.   We shrink
Not from the labor, but we sink
  Beneath its load.   We so deceive

Ourselves and let a vain conceit
  Unsettle reason and betray
What of contentment here we meet
Within this life so brief and fleet
  In the sweet passage of its day.

Incongruous are desires.   We feel
  What it were best we should not do:
We do not all things wise.   We steel
Our hearts against the soft appeal
  Of gentleness and love; we rue

lt to the end, and curse the day
   We harkened to the siren voice
Of base Ambition, to betray
Our happiness and lead us 'way
   From what was far a better choice.

Still move we to its nod, and strive
   For all its vanities as though
They virtue had to keep alive
The soul itself, and seize and hive
   The shadows we pursue to know!

The child aspires to be a man,
   And man aspires to be a god;
They both conspiring 'gainst the plan
Of nature which doth rightly span
   Desires of every earthly clod.

Remote the end will ever be
   We vainly thus pursue and hail;
And that which lures us on we see
Is some mirage of dream, and we
   Are struggling on to sink and fail!

XV.

Ambition mounts a prancing steed!
   No jaded Pegasus can soar
With Genius which is full of greed
And labors only for the deed
   That proves its kindred here below!

We must ascend unto the sky ;
  Give wings to higher thoughts and creeds.
Teach hearts and wills how to deny
The wantonness of earth and fly
  Beyond confines of evil deeds.

How much of pain, how much of toil,
  Is wrought by some ambitious aim,
The zest and humor to recoil
Upon the head which thought to foil
  Conditions that the fates proclaim?

The Catos and the Cæsars fell,
  And Bourbon rule and Spanish sway :
Each page of history can tell
Of man or nation that would swell
  A clamor if but for a day !

Diogenes within his tub
  Was one man in a thousand who
Could here resist the world's hubbub,
And speak to Fame as Beelzebub,
  And tell it of its wild ado ;

And that its aim was vanity ;
  Its doing naught of any worth ;
That peace alone was true degree,
And mild content the sanity,
  That measures wisdom of this earth.

A greater conquerer was he
  Than Alexander by whose arm
The world lay prone.   Alas that we
With that philosopher could see
  That sunshine gives each heart its charm.

And yet each day will make a grave
  Of hope whose pinions were too weak
To buoy ambition on the wave
Of clamor when its god but gave
  It strength enough to rise and seek !

XVI.

Contrast with all the greatness past
  The satisfaction of its hour ;
Some reminiscences will last
And flitful shadows dimly cast —
  The cost was felt in pride of power !

Napoleon came upon the stage —
  Napoleon of a day's renown !
To him man was an open page ;
He marked his passions to engage
  Their force to vault him to a crown !

He made men puppets to his name ;
  He moved each one as though a pawn ;
The goal of all his life was fame,
A chess-board strife ambition's game ;
  And nations fell—their kings to fawn !

He knew man's weakness and he wrought
  His greatness at the fool's expense;
Confiding in his heart the thought
"Through fear and interest all are caught"—*
  His fellows slaves in recompense!

In recompense for strife and blood;
  For hardships borne and labor lost;
For wreck and ruin; ensanguined flood
That swept proud Honor's flag in mud, —
  Repaying so ambition's cost!

In after years Bourriennes to tell
  The secret motives of the great;
Barras to slander and compel
Some confirmation from the well
  Informed—the Talleyrands of State!

Reward? O man, an history's page!
  A mention and a moral, then
Our own affairs our thoughts engage
And with light trifles battles wage —
  The hero's fame forgot again!

XVII.

So was it ever thus.   But still
  We struggle in ambition's strife
For end beyond our feeble skill;
While blank futility doth fill   -
  The briefness of our little life!

---

* "'Fear and interest are the only motives of man,' said Napoleon."—Bourrienne.

We struggle and we fret, to fall
    The victims of our own conceit;
We labor but to taste the gall
That comes with vanity's recall
    When we have faced each lie and cheat.

A wild Bucephalus one mounts
    Where many fall beneath his feet;
The plaudit of the one recounts
The obstacles that he surmounts —
    We crown him with our own defeat!

We give him adulation, but
    'Tis tinged with jealousy and hate!
We mock his actions, call a strut
His gait, and, Cassius like, would cut
    His honor in our own debate!

And this is all the honor comes
    Of mounting mighty things of fame:
A little clamor from the slums;
A crown for Envy's sneer that sums
    The little time bequeaths a name!

XVIII.

The great must ever live afar:
    The eye is keen to see the fault
Of him who rises through the law
That measures genius to debar
    The mediocre with his halt:

When man is with us breast to breast,
  His labor seen beside our own,
His power is ne'er full confest,
Since, arm to arm, we give the test,
  To let our jealousy dethrone.

So distance and the lapse of time,
  Must ever add to glory's star;
Each age and nation, every clime,
Will hold a memory sublime
  That had its being low and far.

The heroes of the past have been
  But pygmies to their fellowmen:
'Tis time alone that shows them kin
To Titans in their strength to win
  The victory denied them then.

XIX.

Move on if there be aught to do!
  Move on though plodding be your gait!
Move on if there be will in you
To find the goal reserved to few;
  For Progress never cares to wait.

Move on and maybe ages hence
  Will cry your glories to the skies;
And, struggling in your own defense
Against the world and its pretense,
  You learn the truth in some vain wise.

Move on! You know the guerdon well,
　And may oblivion find ere long!
Move on and let some other tell
What troubles here his hopes befell,
　And lisp his melancholy song!

That song which told of action spent,
　And toil that added trouble to
The moments claimed by rest, and bent
The head in sorrow while content
　Was lost in vanity's ado:

For soon or late you'll find this true,
　And idle all ambition's strife,
And that the world is full of rue
To everyone who hopes to do
　Something of moment in this life.

XX.

The sage who wrote of Rasselas,
　Warned man of hope's credulity;
Told him that to a lowly pass
Come all vain aims : and proof, alas,
　The ages give in verity!

Who thinks that future time will crown
　Ambitions of his daily toil,
Lives in conceit! A name's renown
Is ever but an empty sound
　That illy pays for life's turmoil.

To-morrow comes the joy to bless!—
    To-day we eke the hour in pain!
Our dreams of bliss and happiness
Awaken ever to distress,
    And all our hopes are futile, vain!

Each day but shows the happy thought
    Was misconceived, and that the heart
In its sweet folly so was caught:
It all resolves itself to naught
    When Time dissolves each feeble part.

Would that the dream could always be;
    The present hold the past, and yet
The pleasures of the future see
Unmarred by pains we pass to be
    The hapless creatures of regret!

XXI.

But let these gloomy thoughts now pass
    With dirges of their dismal train:
Ambition is a cheat, alas!
And peace comes not to any class
    Who find their labors are in vain.

We'll turn us to another scene
    And see what better comes of that.
We'll stray us in the woodland green
And dream of beauties we have seen,
    Within some lone and vine-grown plat.

We'll stray like nature's children true,
  Despite the frets that bar our way;
A freedom is beneath the blue
Found not in domiciles of rue
  Where fierce contention holds the sway.

And then, withal, the country brings
  The out-door sports that recreate;
And from the first warm breath that springs
Till tear-drop of the autumn clings
  An icicle of winter's fate,

The heart of man to nature turns
  And claims relationship in love;
And wall-confinements then it spurns,
And for wild freedom ever yearns
  And seeks the umbral woodland cove

To lose itself and thoughts as well,
  Within the tangled copse and vine,
And be as one with things that dwell
Within the woods; and let that swell
  With rapture which was wont to pine.

With rod and boat on drifting stream,
  Or dog and gun in fenny lands,
The matted shade and sunny beam
Lend romance to our placid dream,
  And help us to forget demands

That Life makes on us every hour;
  For social functions bring us naught
That has not some contentious power
To stir or threaten or to cower
  The will, or man's more daring thought.

XXII.

The sighing, crying, laughing Spring
  That shakes and blows the budding flowers,
Brings Summer on its restless wing,
And then Apollo down doth fling
  His scorching rays to drink the showers;

And earth sleeps 'neath a blazing sky,
  And sultry steals old Auster's breath:
Within the shady groves I lie
And watch with drowsy, listless, eye
  The shimmer on the sun-bathed heath.

I see beyond the rising knoll
  That bares its crown to summer sheen,
And lazy revery fills my soul
With dreams beyond my thoughts' control,
  And bare the spirit world, I ween.

Behold I nymphs and sylphs at play
  As though in Arcady I muse
And here the haunt of elf and fay,
And this Love's own perennial day
  Wherein no pleasure gods refuse.

My soul's transported with the spell
   That comes with knowledge of this bliss;
I here forget the earth to dwell
In bright empyreal realms that swell
   Emotion's metamorphosis,   .

And, like a child in wild pursuit
   Of butterfly that flits its grasp,
I chase each thought that might confute
My dream — to hear the fancied flute
   Of Pan, though he elude my clasp!

In thus beholding mythic sights
   Evanishment is sterner life;
My soul is free and in its flights
It mingles with the fabled wights
   That live within an epic strife.

Will man then wreck this paradise,
   Or try explain the subtle dream?
Is not the pleasure felt suffice
To pay full recompense and price
   For what in fact can only seem?

O dryads! O fair nymphs of trees!
   I love you and your wilds would share!
Your cheerful laughter wakes the bees
And stirs again the slumbering breeze
   That halted in the summer's glare.

XXIII.

The summer's glare that parches earth
    And seres fair Thallo in her bloom;
That dries the springs which babble mirth;
That ripens Carpo in her dearth,
    So wasting all Life would consume:

Then nature droops and pleads for rain,
    The pitiless clouds reflecting heat;
And bird and beast in woods remain,
Cicadas stridulating pain,
    To pipe and die for some retreat.

So is the want of man unfilled
    Within this halting place called home;
And if his struggles here be willed,
His hands to labor are unskilled
    Though death is futile labor's sum!

And here is born the rankling doubt
    That godly care for all provides;
We see withal inglorious rout
Of living forces in the bout
    Waged with Destruction's sweeping tides.

And then a thing of Chance we guess
    Each impulse and the end it brings;
And when a Force we must confess,
'Tis one insensible and less
    A Being than the flux of things!

Malthusian are the laws of life,
   And Want doth ever check increase;
A Darwin sees within such strife
Conditions so selecting life
   The ill-adapted gasp and cease!

XXIV.

But why contend and break our rest
   In reconciling here a fact
With erring faith, thus spurring zest
To the support of what were best
   Forgotten in each life's compact?

The thoughts aweary leave the head,
   With troubles fill the longing heart;
Can not some earthly joy be led
To fill the heart of man instead
   And prove a benefactor's part?

O Groves, within your depths let sleep
   Come weigh my weary eye-lids down:
Let naught disturb me in the deep,
And vigils o'er my slumbers keep
   And hide from me each trouble's frown!

And Sleep, what charms come with thy sway!
   And with what subtleness thy drowse
Steals o'er the being to allay
The wild emotions that the day
   Within the soul doth here arouse?

If thou art brother sure of Death,
  Then Death must be a blessing, too;
For how could likeness of thy breath,
Which soothes tired nature, prove a death
  Whose object is to all undo?

True blessings both when weary Life
  Would lay aside its burdens here,
And there would come surcease of strife
And end of all things that keep rife
  The diabolic dreams of fear.

Then whatsoever bringeth sleep,
  Or lulls the slumberer to rest,
Is thing to bless and not to weep:
And here rapt Solitude doth creep
  On me, and I am truly blest!

Sweet charm of Solitude, I find
  In thee reward of all my toil:
What if man's fetters once could bind
His will? to freedom, unconfined,
  It comes at last in the recoil.

XXV.

It leads us back to other days
  That were not burdened with a care;
It opens to us fitter ways
In which to wend the terrene 'maze
  That here environs all that's fair.

O happy days of sport and ease
    When Youth and Innocence are free.
And jocund Love beneath the trees
Would fond Reciprocation tease,
    Or woo a coy affinity;

When timid eyes confess a tale
    The bashful tongue could never tell;
When dreams of brighter worlds prevail
To shed their luster o'er each vale
    That Gloom would darken with its spell;

When age is but a promised time
    For freer love's enjoyment,
And life is but a lingering prime
Full of the melody and chime
    Of chords that waken heart's content:

When earth and sea and heaven's dome.
    And every grotto found therein,
Is to some one a blissful home,
For flippant Fancy's merry roam,
    And not a dreary waste of sin.

XXVI.

In after life these thoughts come back
    To halo shadows with their light;
We tread again each happy track
And find much pleasure though we lack
    A confirmation of the sight.

An hour's dream can live for aye
  Although it want wise faith and hope;
It leaves within the soul a ray
That brightens many a gloomy day
  That otherwise had barren scope.

Could man's environs ever be
  The drapery of his conceit,
Could fancy live forever free,
Unconscious of mortality
  And what distempers here would mete,

'Twould be an act of infamy
  Unworthy one of tender heart,
To open eyes a grief to see
That here would otherwise be free
  To revel out a happy part.

XXVII.

The days may come, the days may go,
  And bring their sunshine or their shade,
To me will memory ever glow
To bring back happy days of yore
  When Youth and Love together played.

Together played and fancied life
  The passage of a boon divine;
The world a paradise and rife
With all the joys of mystic strife
  That weave Life's web to wind and twine

Affections in the woof of all
  That clothes the naked heart of man
And keeps it warm within its thrall,
Yet binds alone its love, withal,
  And makes it servile to God's plan.

With age comes tendency to drift
  From what in youth the heart would prize;
And cares o'erhang and rarely shift
To let a sun-ray through the rift
  To warm the chill of social ties.

When hearts are young they can not see
  What thorns beset the paths of life;
They grasp at time too eagerly;
They know not what the day will be,
  Nor what is free of toil and strife.

XXVIII.

The youths of either sex are wild
  To taste of liberty and age;
They put aside, with treason mild,
The thoughts and habits of the child,
  And rush to sterner toils engage.

Their pride is in each mark that shows
  The budding of maturity;
The will is set, the heart o'erflows
For share of those same human woes
  The adult cries in misery!

And, full of fire, they will not think,
    But rather choose to ride the tide
Of dalliance, e'en to the brink
Of ruin — but to quaff the drink
    That passion's chalice holds to pride?

Could wisdom ever call a halt
    To race whose goal is meritless,
There had been lives without a fault;
There had been races where the halt
    Was premiumed with a happiness.

XXIX.

But while the youth would hasten time
    In the pursuit of happiness,
The adult weeps a speeding prime,
And age deplores each striking chime
    That tells of dissolution's press:

For with this race and tide of things,
    This nameless longing for the will
And freedom of each wish, time brings
Reward we wot not of and wrings
    The heart with vainer longings still.

So Age must look upon the whim
    Of Youth with scorn of its desire;
For while life's chalice here is brim
With health and love, the end is dim;
    Or lost to sight by ardor's fire.

XXX.

O woman, in thy maid-blush pause!
  Short is the span from Youth to Age,
And stern is nature and her laws;
She will resent the slightest cause
  That mars a day's recorded page.

Thy youth at best is but a day;
  Thy rosiness ephemeral;
Thy smile is but a flitting ray
To light thy face and then away
  By some grim law satanical:

Thy pride is but a foolish mark
  For archers of thy destiny;
Thy conscious thoughts are rendered stark;
Thy fancy soars but as a spark
  That dies in its impotency.

Thy span is short; for school days done,
  Dame Fashion urges thee in life;
And so that blush, so new begun,
Is faded in vain folly's run,
  Or thou art some poor plodder's wife!

Thy freshness gone ere life is blown
  Into the mellowness of day;
Or maybe child to matron grown
Ere wisdom is or age hath shown
  The ripeness that comes with delay.

And Art is called to lend its aid
  In patching up a lame machine ;
And what was once a blooming maid
Is soon a butterfly of trade
  That fades and flutters in its teen !

A butterfly that flits a day
  In realms of fancy pilotless :
In thee man finds his willing prey,
Since thou art set the spoiler's way
  And left alone in helplessness !

XXXI.

Yea, Woman is Man's wage and prey,
  His luring goal, his mad desire,
His passion's rage, his power's sway
That lets no curb him halt, or stay
  The blood of lust when set on fire.

The very force in him doth move
  As by magnetic charm, and he
Is fierce and eager in his love,
And scorns restraints it would behoove
  Them both observe in truancy.

A Woman's strength is in her worth,
  And not within a sensual deed ;
'Twere pity God should give her birth
To be a wanton on the earth
  To bear and leave a worthless breed.

Her office is of love and cheer,
  Of sweet companionship to man ;
She sure to all the world were dear
Should she deport herself with care
  And lighten sorrows as she can.

XXXII.

Yet she but faintly sees, withal,
  And trusts, perhaps. where faith is sin ;
A lonely soul can not recall
Affections though they may enthrall
  The better sentiments within.

Man's love is like a comet come
  Within the sky of woman's sphere ;
A flash, a pleasing smile like some
Strange Sun that flings his glory's sum
  In radiance around her there !

His orbit's dark, but tongue is sweet
  And knows the lore of flattery's art :
She trembles in her plane to meet
The fond caresses of his greet,
  And gives for promises her heart !

But she as planet here is hung
  With an ecliptic that is known ;
Herself defined by Gossip's tongue ;
Her every fault and failing sung
  By every idle breath that's blown !

Still unknown may that lover be
    And black in heart as any Cain :
In night Romance can better see
Materials for its phantasy
    And dight aright its grotesque train.

A sun is but a guess at best,
    A comet but a trail of light ;
The one, as wearied, sinks to rest
And leaves the heart sick in its quest ;
    The other scampers in the night!

XXXIII.

In lieu she learns of quibs and art,
    And practices a mild deceit ;
And seeks to hide a wanton heart,
And tries to play a careless part
    With rank intent to fraud and cheat :

She nurses in her soul the thought
    That some hypocrisy may win ;
But oft in her own trap is caught
And all her wiles conceived for naught,
    Or, worse, to steep her heart in sin.

And beauty, if by nature not,
    She seeks to paint upon her cheek,
To friz it in her hair, or blot
It somewhere in a " beauty-spot " —
    To make herself a blazoned freak !

She fills a bad form out to give
　　You Hebe lines by tailor's art;
She ambles, graces, makes believe,
And fondly smiles but to deceive —
　　To play with man an equal part!

XXXIV.

A little game in life we play
　　In passing through its fleeting span;
A little game, which, true to say.
Is not just what we honor, nay,
　　A game we play confounding man!

A little game of lie to cheat
　　A confidence new born of trust;
A little game for faith's defeat;
A game for mockery's repeat
　　To prove sincerity accurst.

Within a bragging age we find
　　These caricatured truths that show
How little comes to man so blind
He can not see the trend and wind
　　Of Falsehood in affairs below!

And so we stumble day by day
　　To fall in snares Deceit has laid,
And all because this vital clay
Is wrong compounded and finds pay
　　In folly through the Devil's trade.

XXXV.

A little game of love to lead
  Some trusting heart into a snare,
A little game of hate to feed
The venom rankling in the seed
  Of life that blossoms in despair:

A little more of falsehood then
  To fill the social state of man
And leave his soul as dark as when
It crouched within its savage den
  Unconscious of its broader span.

The instinct of the brute is still
  The moral guide of not a few,
And uncontrolled the savage will,
And bent to selfishness until
  The lair's ethics homes imbrue!

We blush to see the smirking lie
  Take full command of heart's control;
We weep to see man's honor die;
But what avails our tear or sigh
  If we debase the human soul?

XXXVI.

He is deceived who lets the eye
  Be judge alone of all the world:
'Tis thus we oft mistake the Lie
And call " an honest man " the sly
  Deceiver who would leave us churled.

Are we traduced by bluntness here,
  Or the palaver of man's speech?
The mannered man we rightly fear
Because his conduct is not clear,
  Nor acts within thought's lazy reach.

Far fairer is the rugged man
  Of uncouth speech and simple ways;
Him and his methods we can scan;
His cruder conduct is the plan
  Of honesty that naught betrays.

XXXVII.

How profitless is all of this!
  We note it but to let it pass!
We'd rather coax some thought of bliss
Than think of life just as it is,
  For conscience to cry out, alas!

'Tis part of life to live in dreams;
  Build castles but to see them fall;
A pleasure is but what it seems,
And he that dwells in fancy's realms
  Knows most of earthly bliss, withal.

I've lived it through and comfort found
  In visions that I knew untrue:
What did I care? I'd rather sound
A pleasure false than feel the wound
  Of hope deferred I thought my due.

It matters not what trend my thought
  Has taken in its wanton flight;
To me the image that is wrought
Is instinct with my life and fraught
  With pleasure, though a passing light.

XXXVIII.

I've had bright visions of a home
  That I might sometime see or know;
Wherein I'd find a sweet welcome
And place to rest, and cease to roam
  About the world with spirit sore:

For mine was e'er a restless soul
  That battered 'gainst its narrow cage;
My thoughts would soar beyond control,
Amid ethereal spheres would roll
  And boundless platitudes engage!

I've had bright dreams, I say: a fair
  And lonely cove 'mid wildest scene;
A cot upon a rugged square
Of mountain ledge, all lone and bare
  Above and capped in glinting sheen,

Below great fertile plains. a sea
  That rolls and swells in majesty.
A silvery stream that ploughs the lea
Meandering lazily to the sea
  To lose itself with murmuring sigh.

'Tis here my restless soul would live
  With all the freedom of the lark;
Amid such grandeur Hope can give
Each pleasure liberty and live
  Again as in the primal spark!

XXXIX.

I've pictured so my home: I'd live
  'Mid balmy winds and babbling streams:
I'd coax the birds their songs to give
To harmonize it all: I'd live
  Forever in my languid dreams!

And what can fairer be than this?
  Or what thing happier to plan
Than dream-life full of happiness?
A region of unbounded bliss
  Born of the wild conceit of man?

For, should I pall, I'd merely try
  The world again, and, sickened, soon
To eyrie back my soul would fly
As bird of wild unrest, to die
  Amidst the comforts of this boon.

'Tis false to think one satisfied
  With what he has of earth; his lot
Is mean when he has once espied
A fellow's, though to him untried—
  'Tis fair because he knows it not!

The weary wanderer seeks a home ;
　　And he beside the hearth-stone longs
For pleasures of an idle roam :
And so from cradle unto tomb
　　Comes discontentment's luring songs.

XL.

I stray alone to view the world,
　　In silence seeking sympathy ;
Ensanguined so my hopes unfurl
To temper spirit of the churl
　　That dwells within my misery :

And thought's conspiracy is dead,
　　And treason in the soul unknown ;
And my unrest is vanquished, fled
Beyond the pale of that it fed,
　　To leave me undisturbed, alone.

And so I revel in the sights
　　Fair nature stretches out to view ;
I people space and see delights
In idle fellowships with wights
　　Unreal and to fancy due.

And thus the dormant soul of man,
　　Full of the charms of life, awakes
And all the range of earth would scan
To find a breadth of love to span
　　The breach that Hell's distemper makes.

XLI.

How beautiful the land and sea,
  And the soft glowing sky above:
The lofty mountains and the lea
That stretches forth to meet and be
  Horizon to the plains of Jove:

How beautiful each life that glows
  To color everything in view;
How beautiful the blushing rose,
And every flowering shrub that shows
  The Spirit which doth all renew.

How beautiful the peaceful day
  And the serenity of night;
How grand the storm that breaks its stay
And thunders o'er the world away
  To wreck within its fury's might:

E'en to the narrow range of man
  Bound to his lot by earthen gyves,
Though humble be his lowly span,
Yet of what grandeur is the plan
  Of everything for which he strives.

How beautiful, how beautiful;
  And yet how strangely, truly sad
That man is here less dutiful
Than any creature beautiful
  That makes or leaves the world so glad!

Yea, true, 'tis man alone's deformed,
  And he that mars the face of earth ;
And he that tortures and is harmed
By his own craft, and yet is armed
  For the destruction of all worth !

He builds and he destroys.   He plays
  With dangerous tools and thinks his deeds
Are wise ; and in this he displays
Noetic brain, perhaps, but ways
  In strange adjustment to his needs.

XLII.

But when beneath the arching skies
  In lonely solitude we roam,
We this forget and let our eyes
Pursue the fleecy cloud that flies
  Within the heaven's azure dome.

Could we but live within that mass
  And hie us in its billowy folds,
The earth and all its rue might pass,
No stricken soul to cry, alas !
  Because of Nature's bites and scolds.

We'd drink the harmony of sound ;
  We'd listen to the lisping wind ;
We'd free ourselves of all that bound ;
We'd feel no earthly jar or wound,
  Nor binding cord that once confined !

We'd be of truest likeness then
　To that we boast, our image is,
Or as the Soul in nature when
Its pristine essence is again
　Resumed to be dissolved in bliss.

XLIII.

To be alone is company,
　As Greek philosophy once said;
And solitude can sometimes be
Amid the gayest company
　If hearts to sober thoughts are wed.

1 needed not this apothegm
　To tell me of a mind's unrest;
I've felt it, and I've tried to stem
My scurring thoughts, or hinder them
　From bringing on a vexing quest.

1 drift myself into the sea
　Of troubles that I would avoid;
I flounder, and my buoyancy
Is sunk by scorn and mockery,
　And all life's pleasures are alloyed!

XLIV.

But still in solitude is charm
　More subtle than the poets say;
For what know they of hearts' alarm?
Or measure of each damning harm
　This solitude can soothe away?

Instinct with dream they only see
　The visions of their ardor born ;
The creatures of wild phantasy ;
The eidolons that can not be,
　Or things of strange Athenic spawn ;

Whilst we, beset with mundane toil
　And struggling in our narrow bounds.
Can feel more keenly life's turmoil,
Embitterment we can not foil,
　To writhe in agony of wounds !

Because we can not speak as they
　In wild and rhythmic rapsody,
Is it the proof of brighter way ?
Or that we stumble in our lay,
　Too full of pain for harmony ?

The deepest grief is dumb of tongue
　And silent is the throb of death,
The pang that has in anguish wrung
Was never to sweet music sung,
　For gasping in its speech and breath.

XLV

But Solitude, O Solitude !
　How sweet to lie and dream with thee !
How gracious is thy voiceless mood.
Thy desert stillness, or the rude,
　Fierce roaring breakers of the sea !

For whether in the plain or wood,
   The mountain or the ocean's calm,
The heart has ever understood
The language of thy pensive flood
   That soothes to rest its wild alarm.

Oppressed with grief to thee would turn
   Each soul for sympathy and rest;
For thou wast never known to spurn
A spirit that could here once yearn
   For that with which thou art so blest.

XLVI.

I love the coves of solitude;
   I love the silent dells and wood;
I love the mountain and the rude
Waves of the beach, their amplitude,
   And the wild dashings of their flood.

I watch the ocean waves and say,
   Thalassa of wild billows, roll!
Within thy froth fair Nereids play,
And Oceanides there spray
   The rainbow of thy wrath's control:

Upon thy bosom ploughs the fleet
   Of man in " golden argosies";
And silver though thy shining sheet,
A slave art thou to traffic feet —
   Leviathan of human prize!

And Neptune or Poseidon eld,
    With trident pricks thy liquid heart,
And leaping dolphins, too, would swell
Their reign, or Nautilus compel
    Thee bear aloft her tiny yacht :

Thou kissest shores remote and near,
    Thou liquid bridge of distant lands!
Thou billow of a Pluvian tear
That fell to water earth when sere,
    And here remained for Life's commands !

We play within thy drifting sands,
    We chase thy tides and ride thy waves ;
We compass thee within our lands,
And dare abuse thy law's commands
    Though yawning are thy swirling graves.

O peaceful Stream that Nereus mild
    Was want to govern in thy flow,
Is power in thee fierce and wild,
Here docile as obedient child
    But to deceive the spirit so ?

Yea, Proteus is thy god as well,
    And changeable art thou as he !
Thy gentle undulating swell
May burst to wreck when none can tell
    What cargos sunk and what at sea !

XLVII.

Thy name, O Ocean, sounds of fame!
  Great Homer wound thee 'round the earth;
Gave thee fair Tethys as thy dame,
And fairer offspring of thy name :
  And all pronounced thee full of worth.

" Thalassa" by the Grecian host,
  "Thalatta" in the Attic tongue,
As waves of thee dashed on the coast
To wreck the things of human boast—
  Of thee onomatope they sung!

But what name fitting to the wail
  That comes with all thy storm and roar?
When in thy seething floods the Sail
Sinks 'neath the billows of thy gale
  That hurl strange fragments on the shore?

XLVIII.

I dreamed of thee and thought I saw
  A Demon sleeping on thy breast :
A Being wraught of nature's flaw,
A hideous Shape defying law,—
  Huge, stretching north and south and west.

His breathing shook thy treacherous calm
  And jarred the pendant heavens high;
And when he moved all felt alarm,
And waves sprang up as though a harm
  Was in their sleeping so near by!

A sail flew o'er the sea and woke
  This monster of the raging deep :
A flashing eye, a lightning stroke.
And thundering billows leaped and broke,
  The frail thing with one fell sweep!

And mocking winds hurled fragments high,
  And drifts were broken on the shore,
And sea-gulls answered human cry,
And storms, deriding, passed on by,
  And sunk debris forever more !—

Thou baffling oceanic Stream,
  Awake not thoughts of storm and rage :
Thou now art calm, so let me dream
Of thee as some smooth, flowing stream
  As in the fair archaic age.

XLIX.

From birth to death this life is change,
  New scenes to dawn with every day ;
Time's fleeting image sure can range
From hour to hour although each strange
  Emotion halts as if to stay :

To-day our hearts are filled with joy,
  To-morrow sorrow ekes the hour ;
And next some pleasure would decoy,
Or drown the troubles that annoy—
  And we the playthings of some Power!

The flying fronds, or sifting sand,
  That drift on winds of Destiny;
The huddled leaves upon the land
Obeying fatuous command
  And swirling till we lifeless lie!

L.

We light upon a certain place
  And for a season call it home;
We leave for each remembered face
To linger in its wonted grace,
  So plaguing thence our aimless roam!

Like birds of passage in their flight,
  We come and go 'mid tempests swell;
Our greeting but a passing light
That lends a radiance for the Night
  To snuff and give us back "farewell"!

And friends forget and deem us dead—
  For Absence is Oblivion's host!
And dreams that were are quickly fled
For newer ties to bind instead
  And leave the heart an empty boast!

LI.

I've seen a little bird uncaged
  That fluttered 'round its prison home:
Uncertain freedom so engaged
Its hope and fear—and so have waged
  Emotion's battles when I roam!

A prison is in Freedom's wild
  Where boundless vistas hove in view;
For vastness renders impulse mild;
Each soaring thought is natures child;
  A home, a joy, is still life's due.

Unsatisfied we strive in vain
  To find some peace and place of rest;
'Tis not in snapping friendship's chain
To wander o'er earth's lonely main
  Companionless that we are blest.

LII.

In solitude the charm we find
  Is living o'er our lives again;
Regaling thought in memory's wind,
Allowing love-hopes so to bind
  All pleasures we would have remain:

See with a different light and eye
  Life's incidents so near forgot;
Recall the times for which we sigh;
Hear songs of joy that drown the cry
  Wailed by the waif of hapless lot.

But solitude and I have dwelt
  Within this clay for, lo, so long!
I know his mood and he has felt
The gloom in me; and such is pelt
  To spirit that gives forth this song.

LIII

" Farewell!" I say to dreams each day :
  Farewell to scenes and friends I've known ;
" Farewell!" and in my feeble way
I try express the throbs that say
  " Farewell" with depths to words unknown!

And yet I'm only half expressed
  And misinterpreted and feared,
And all my heart has e'er confessed
Was disbelieved, or deemed the test
  Of baseness that the cynic stirred!

Yet still I turn to say " farewell "
  Though doubt may mock sincerity ;
I can not, will not, break the spell
That binds the past ; I hence would dwell
  In realms of cherished memory.

LIV.

I love to hold a memory sweet,
  I love to dream of pleasures past ;
I love for pictures to repeat
Conceptions to old Time's defeat
  And stamp impressions that will last :

I cherish them and, miser like,
  Would gloat o'er their possession aye ;
I hoard each vision that can strike
The sympathetic chord I like
  To sound its melody each day :

And so within safe keeping I
  Hold much the world may deem as dross,
And with love's tenderness and eye,
I touch, and see, and, loving, sigh
  For what may better be my loss!

LV.

The pictures I have laid away
  Are not Daguerreotypes of art;
Nor chiseled in some wasting clay;
But photographed by finer ray
  On sensor-tablets of my heart.

No magic sibyl ever held
  Had half the power of these to bring
The joys back that once compelled
The heart to worship, or that swelled
  The overflow of youth's bright spring.

I live again the moments through
  As though no day had spaced my love;
I feel a fellowship as true
As any that life ever knew—
  Though answering spirit may not move.

Enough it is to feel the bliss
  And know the dream is ever young;
That Toil and Age the brow may kiss,
But naught can prove the heart remiss
  That holds an image Fancy sprung.

LVI

In train a myriad visions stand
   Like sylphs in fairy-land of dream;
Each holds a love at its command;
Each waves submission by its hand;
   Each is, though it may only seem!

It is, for by its subtle power
   It frees oppression of my thought,
And, in the transport of its hour,
It sweeps the soul with magic power
   To purge it of what frenzy wrought.

LVII.

My school-day's love I can't deny,
   Nor how my sentiments would flow
When under trees I used to lie
And dream the future o'er and sigh
   For that I never was to know.

For, school-days done, I drifted on
   To other scenes and other loves,
For them in turn to leave upon
My mind impressions that will run
   To end of memory's sportive roves.

Though sweetheart of my boyhood days
   Could scarcely move affections now,
I can not yet forget her ways,
Or here deny that she still plays
   The wanton with my heart, somehow!

LVIII.

I see a maid bare-footed, tanned,
  But beauty in both form and face;
She trips across the new plowed land
While from her small and sun-burnt hand,
  She drops the grain where furrows lace:

Her eyes are bright with youthful fire,
  Her hair with sunlight frolic mad,
Her step is agile and desire
Would burn her cheeks when eyes admire
  The rounded limbs so scantly clad.

She is to me a mountain fay!
  A wandering Knight I am to her!
A sweet romance with each would play—
I hold the vision, but the day
  Is past to leave me but its cheer!

LIX

I see a lady proud and grand,
  With beauty that transcends a star;
She greets and smiles: I lose command
Of heart and will, and, trembling, stand
  A suppliant pleading at love's bar!

She leads me hither, thither, ways
  I dare not here confess because
'Twould show how weak the strongest stays
We boast! The misanthrope obeys
  The promptings of some social laws!

The real passes and the dream
  Is all I have to mark the day.
I only know what love did seem :
I would not shatter fancy's realm
  By searching deeper in the play.

LX.

So seasons bring their gifts, and pain
  Of parting ere true friendship's ripe :
Blue eyes or brown, in happy train
Flash on my life to leave again,
  And I retain a passing type!

I care not? Yes; though knowledge sees
  All semblance of the real destroyed!
I'd rather pass my life with these
And feel their warmth than know the freeze
  That chills the hopes of all enjoyed.

'Twill vanish soon enough although
  We hold each shadow as divine :
The truth contains much human woe :
We can not always see the glow
  Of life when suffering in its pine.

LXI.

On moieties we live and thrive,
  On shadows base our love and faith ;
We hope and dream and ever strive
To keep our feeble flame alive
  Though aimless as a shadow-wraith.

And these with recollections vain
　Wove in the fabric of each life,
Defy Arachne's art again
To show the world a gayer train
　Spun of her wild and fabled strife.

'Tis dreaming thus that poets find
　The fair creations of their verse,
And let their brooding thoughts combine
In rhythmic cadences divine
　The treasures of the mental purse.

And so we know, in sober truth,
　The creature of each frenzied mind
Is one in fancy bred; insooth,
An apparition of the Truth
　That longings of the heart would bind;

And that it isn't half so fair
　As phantasy would make believe;
But seen within the light of care,
We find its virtues strangely rare—
　For 'tis Love's province to deceive!

As some one has so aptly said,
　The most adorable is she
Whom we have never met, nor wed
To fickle thought to turn the head
　A moment from reality.

The wise will always love and sigh;
   The foolish only live in bliss!
When buoyant hopes would soar too high
Reflection shows the sham and lie
   That are one half of all that is!

LXII.

How happy must the yeoman be
   Amid his fields and feeding flocks,
Where nature's rare simplicity
Is mirrowed in the sky and lea,
   And even ruggedness of rocks.

No passions stir his bosom's calm,
   Fraught of the wrangle of his kind;
He views the world without alarm;
Sees pleasures in each sylvan charm,
   And happiness with all combined:

He plows his lands, he sows his grain,
   And reaps a harvest for his toil;
He tends his herds upon the plain;
Or drives the jolly, rumbling wain
   For products of the fertile soil:

His cares are as the springtime cloud—
   A passing shadow and no more:
An ill the sunshine has allowed
To sweep his soul; a shifting cloud
   That drops a tear in flitting so!

His prancing steeds, his lowing kine
  That feed within the meadows green,
His lambs agambol and the swine
That bask within the warm sunshine
  So rendering picturesque the scene;

The chirping birds, the chanticleer
  That crows its freedom to the soul;
The swans afloat on silver mere,
The plough-boy's happy song of cheer—
  These are the joys of his control.

The morning finds him up and out
  With sunlight and the sparkling dew;
Fresh nature's glowing air about
Invigorating life to rout
  The ills that languidness would brew;

At noon the blast of horn recalls
  The passing day and nature's need;
Within the shade of trees he sprawls,
And drowsily his mind recalls
  Each season's winnowings of seed.

At eve when sun is sinking red,
  He wends him home in tuneful joy;
At night he seeks his humble bed,
No thoughts tormenting heart or head,
  And sleeps to dream of love's employ.

LXIII.

Contrast with this the city life
  With all its bustle and its roar ;
Its howling greed, its angry strife
That tramples down each feeble life
  Which vainly struggles to the fore ;

Its brawling crime and snarling death ;
  Its cries of want and wild despairs ;
Its dust and smoke which stifle breath ;
Its foul effluvia of death ;
  Its catacombs of human lairs ;

Its seed of whirlwind, crop of tares ;
  Its hells of woe, its devils' care ;
Its folly-shops of sham-faced wares ;
Its tolls, its panders and its snares—
  And these are what we can compare !

Miasmas fill its alley ways,
  And Want is fellow of the hour ;
And Life a Life to ills betrays,
And with Contagion foully plays
  For Death, the unrelenting Power :

And some inventive Genius springs
  A trap for Riches to ascend ;
A trap that to the many brings
A fall and downward slope of things
  By making much on one depend :

The lazzaroni of the street
  Are mocks of sympathy and wealth;
And Opulence, with noisy feet,
Would drown the cries which might repeat
  The tales told of its adroit stealth!

How much was robbed and how much earned
  By honest labor of the hand?
How much had better nature spurned
The methods of increase which turned
  " An honest penny's " base command?

LXIV.

And yet the Youth on entering life
  Is taught that power waits on wealth;
Not that pursuit brings weary strife,
Possession sodidness of life
  And pains attending wasted health.

He's driven into business cares
  That bow his head, corrupt his heart:
And promised but a goal that fears
Its exaltation and the sneers
  Of those who know its crafty art;

The art that Honesty disdains
  As stepping stone of Fraud and Lie;
The art that Artifice maintains
And never purpose base restrains
  Though end be in a fellow's cry.

And so the fairest mark of pride
  Is graven on a gilded shaft
That tells how sympathy has died
And better purpose been denied
  For base devices of a craft!

LXV.

The greatest curse of man to-day
  Is love of gold and its pursuit;
The littleness that holds the sway
Of wills within their wily play,
  To leave conditions of the brute!

I hold it that a heart when set
  On this pale drudge of avarice,
Is prone to any crime abet
Which clears the way or helps to let
  An object pass for its increase:

And from the first when cattle meant
  Pecunia of ancestral trade,
The *pecus* stood for vile intent
To seize, and hold aggrandizement
  The aim of every barter made:

And even now when man would boast
  Enlightenment and moral eye,
His traffic is the same in cost
As that which moved the barbarous host;
  His betterment a vanity!

LXVI.

Young Hermes, Grecian god of Trade,
  Was god as well of Theft and Lie;
'S tho' theft and lie the traffic made,
Or barter little truth displayed,
  Or honor showed within its ply!

This god was likewise god of Speech;
  Inventive source of Cadmean sign!
Speech for the wily tongue to teach
The will to make a moral breech
  That promised profit by its whine!

What wonder then a custom born
  Of such a source should find an end
In that alone which foster scorn,
Which teaches mankind how to fawn
  To Powers that on wealth depend?

LXVII.

It is a trait of humankind—
  Born with us in the savage state—
To entertain a grasping mind
That hopes in someway here to find
  The treasures it doth meditate.

Mistaken are we all and blind
  To truths of life as time will show;
The good of that we hope to find
Is lost within the maze and wind
  Of byways Greed entangles so.

Wealth is not sum of happiness,
   Nor power measure of desire,
Nor worldly splendor all of bliss,
Nor charm of all in what we miss,
   Nor love alone in sensual fire ;

Some spice must season everything
   And render palatable sweets
Which cloy in surfeit ; so to bring
The human taste to earthly thing
   And clear the mind of its conceits.

LXVIII.

Return again unto the scene
   Of rural innocence and peace :
If soul be weary touch the green,
Antæus-like, it will be seen
   To strengthen with the earth's increase !

We all were woodland fauns, perhaps,
   Before we yoked ourselves as men ;
Before we forged deceitful traps
For human frailties and mishaps,
   Or tempted dolts in social pen.

Before we fettered docile wills
   To labor in our selfish use ;
Before we knew inventive skills,
Or dreamed of subjugating wills
   To their betrayal and abuse.

We boast of freedom, to enslave
   Each helpless thing that comes in way!
Unmanumitted souls but crave
The freedom God to others gave—
   Enslaved themselves by passion's sway.

We fetter selves and teach our hands
   To forge the fetters of our dupes;
A gaoler-den we make all lands,
And proudly strut and give commands,
   And brag of dumb-voiced, servile, troops!

LXIX.

Yea, freedom is in being free
   To make a hell of all the world,
And letting human avarice be
The master passion, and the plea
   Of all the baseness of the churl!

And fairness is in being fair
   When power is to here restrain;
Or, 'tis in taking major share
Of everything for which we care
   When no one dares bid us refrain!

And justice is the thing we boast
   When we have neither want nor will
To gratify, and all the cost
Is borne by others, or is lost
   In test of some one's poorer skill.

LXX.

Born free we are : Equality
　Is not a thing of birth, but worth.
'Tis stuff that makes the man ; degree
Of elements arranged to be
　Perchance a power on the earth.

Some move this way and some move that—
　These children in their passions blind.
Those as though some divine fiat
Predestined them to conquer that
　Which blocks the way of dull mankind.

By prejudice and passion moved
　The vast majority of men :
Throw off restraint and it is proved
All are but creatures it behooved
　The wiser to restrain and pen !

Anarchial in both thought and mood,
　Destructive and of social flaw ;
Some Reason has to stir and brood,
Devise a means and rule of good
　And force the regnancy of law !

LXXI.

We've mocked the nature love confest ;
　We've scorned the pristine chaim and sway ;
We've filled our souls with fierce contest
To baffle all the dreams of rest ;
　We're authors of our own dismay :

We're moved to purpose and design
    The god-like in us must deplore;
We've set a gait and marked a sign
That generations may repine
    In reaping what our errors sow:

And social state that promised peace
    In plea for strength which it combined,
Has turned the force for ills increase,
Or for Contention's greater lease
    In bringing struggles on mankind.

LXXII.

So Aristotle's postulate
    That man was born a citizen,
Is called in question here of late,
And, by new canons of debate,
    He's found the creature of a den!

And if a *polites* at all,
    A ramping, howling, " diplomat "
Whose social state is one of gall,
The " citizen," " political;"—
    Transforming *polites* to that!

Was ever word so misconstrued,
    Or misinterpreted by use?
A term of fellowship for feud!
A word whose meaning would include
    Within itself its own abuse!

We find, indeed, the " citizen,"
   Instead of being neighbor true,
Is oftener a partizan
Whose business is to cheat, and plan
   The robbing of another's due ;

And that his " patriotism " is
   What surly Johnson would define :
A scoundrel's apt lip-word in his
Defense of his own act remiss,
   Or the disguise of his design.

Yet " politics " is still the cant
   Of those who prate of polity ;
Of demagogue and sycophant,
And " statesmen " far more ignorant
   Of statecraft than diplomacy !

LXXIII.

'Tis plain that if we view mankind
   In any light our reason knows,
A tugging, fudging, mass we find
Of divers aims, and, passion blind,
   Each holding all the rest as foes !

In toils of rancor, din of sound,
   Most labors seem but to estrange ;
Yet each is stung by selfish wound,
Which shows that all are linked and bound
   By some concatenation strange.

LXXIV.

Society, Society
  To what condition is thy name?
Once stood the term for God's decree
Spoke to the soul's affinity
  That it wild impulses might tame.

From primal germ of savage state
  Art thou advanced or lower borne?
Thy wisdom holdeth yet debate
With some instincts that here relate
  Thee to a former plain of scorn.

And baser ends thy humors crave
  Than Troglodytes conceived withal;
For in the more exalted " cave "
That union built, thy freedom gave
  A license for thy social thrall!

Now man is moved by thy decrees,
  And virtue loses through thy claims,
Whilst Wealth holds greatest power to please,
And Sham enjoys fullest ease—
  The tenor of thy vaunted aims!

And is this what was promised when
  All gave their aid to help thee bind
The social tie that was to pen
The wild community of men
  Into the noble caste " Mankind "?

LXXV.

Society, Society,
  What dignity canst thou confer?
The state of nature, wild and free,
Is dignity to what we see
  Exampled in thy social leer.

The man who once found pride in truth,
  And scorned dissemblings of the lie,
Is now seduced, and from his youth
Is taught the lesson of thy ruth—
  Himself deceived to falsify!

We speak of savage red-man found
  Within this land which we call ours;
We let not honest truth confound
Our pride by telling how we hound'd
  A truer nature by our powers.

He brought a calmuet of peace;
  A faith conceiving us divine!
We, "fire-water" to increase
His ills; a "forked-tongue's" release
  In proof of our "benign" design!

His Manitou we soon despised,
  And forced a faith beyond his ken;
We haggled and deceived, devised
New tortures for his hurt, reprised
  His lands and slew his people, then—

Our mission was of love, we say !
   Our faith a civilizing force !
The savage is our helpless prey ;
Evangelizing him we may
   Enlighten so the world—of course !

Teach him the morals sprung of lie !
   The virtue of hypocrisy !
The love of profit, and the sigh
Born of our selfishness ; the cry
   Of clamorous frivolity.

LXXVI.

Society !   Society !
   When earth was young and man was new,
His soul knew no obscurity ;
His lowly intellect was free
   Of Speculation's wise ado.

No dreaming *Nous* pronounced him damn'd
   Because of goblins in his mind ;
No mystic microcosm spann'd
Hiatus of a god's command
   To find a Hell if he was blind !

His dream was real, his pleasures sweet,
   Untrubled by a code of ill ;
He paired as birds pair, his retreat
Was home and full of all things meet
   For simple happiness of will.

Was Rome more happy than wild Gaul
    Whose peoples lived in huts of straw?
She rolled in wealth and vice, withal,
But could not e'en so much as call
    Her soul her own by will or law!

Peace hung upon a tyrant's smile;
    It trembled at his passing nod;
And virtue was a thing of guile,
Defloured for an idle while
    As though a luckless gift of God!

The shrineless gods of German host
    Dealt fairer with their devotees:
No chambered temples could they boast,
Nor altars smoking with lamb's roast,
    But virtue dwelt among the trees.

The dames of lusty warriors sprung
    Like Spartan matrons to the fight;
They helped the lordly arm and sung
Encouragement, and, chastely clung
    To all that was in honor right.

They bartered not themselves nor gave
    Their lieges any cause for shame:
Their duties were to tend and save,
In battles fierce, the fallen brave,
    Or keep alive his honored name.

Well might a Tacitus cry out,
  Comparing them to sensual drones
Of Romish ease, whose silly pout
Was love's device, a ruse for lout,
  A voice inveigling in its tones!

LXXVII.

Society, Society,
  Art thou advanced on Gothic creeds?
Ah, Jezebels are born of thee,
And Sensuality is free
  To mark thy progress with its deeds!

The savage virtues are debased
  For social Sybarites to reign,
And style of Artemis defaced,
Or by Astarte now replaced
  For base Propœtic love again.   .

An age that brags of chivalry
  And equal rights to either sex,
Decadence shows in parity,
And not the progress faith would see
  Wraught by the social part's contex!

Disdain for manly qualities
  Marks everything effeminate;
A languor born of wanton ease
Is humor which perhaps may please
  A feeble mind's more feeble state.

LXXVIII.

Society, Society,
  Who forced on woman sin and shame,
And filled her head with vanity,
And taught her inutility
  In that for which she bears the blame?

Thy fashions wrecked a graceful form
  And hugged diseases in their grip;
Thy arts to maiden's blush did harm;
Thy manners lost her simple charm
  And stole the truth from eye and lip!

She ogles and denies, and plays
  The hoiden to a soubrette's taste;
And by false acts the heart betrays
That beats for her, and breaks the stays
  That bind the sacred married state!

As Rousseau charged of old, she gives
  Her babe into a nurse's care;
Disports herself, and, if it lives,
A fine example then she gives
  Of how the meretricious fare!

LXXIX.

Society! Society!
  In lieu of consort that proclaims
Our sires' superiority,
We hold concupiscence is free
  To here embrace its sensual aims!

Conjugal state is social woe :
   The bachelor and " bachelor-maid,"
Are evolutions come before
The Freeloveism we may know
   When lawful wedlock is delayed.

Delayed to let the passions sway
   The will to fancies of an hour ;
Delayed to let hot lust betray
The head and turn its thoughts away
   From sequence of a venal power.

And this we call Advancement now :
   This low incontinance and lust !
And acts untoward we allow,
While vain imaginings somehow
   Prove false to each misguided trust.

Great Shakespeare truly understood
   These little weaknesses of man ;
His imp of satire wisely could
Discern each temperment of good,
   And see each crafty devil's plan.

'Tis no less true of ages past
   Than of the present which we see ;
And what Puck said will ever last
Man's verdant vanity to blast,
   With, " O what fools these mortals be "!

LXXX.

Society! Society!
  To quibble, jest, with idle tongue,
And show a mental vacancy,
Is all the lesson learned of thee
  To soothe the pang of conscience rung

By thy decrees and wilful acts
  Which license mischief in mankind;
The soul conceives of what it lacks
By thy disparagement of facts,
  And by thy feebleness of mind.

From youth to manhood's eager prime
  The passions are within thy school,
And modesty is deemed a crime
That dims the luster of the time,
  Since frolic is the sanctioned rule:

And early in the day is taught
  Thy light frivolity of will,
And spirit of presumption caught,
And act of indescretion's thought
  That moves but to accomplish ill.

LXXXI.

Society, Society,
  Where rest the faults of thy estate?
Who turned the social impulse free
And taught it how to wreck and be
  A farce for empty fools' debate?

'Tis not so easy to undo
　An error as to teach a vice :
A thought deep-rooted is as true
To him who holds it as the due
　Of any act or sage advice.

Who then will stand for vicious deed,
　Disgrace and social turpitude?
Society hath sown the seed,
Society will reap the weed
　Grown in its own base servitude !

LXXXII.

What gilded halls of wreck and sin
　Wherein the flowing bowl is passed,
And where the die is cast to win
Or lose the fortunes chanced within
　That wiser moments have amassed ;

What clinking glasses of champagne
　And wines of amber or of red,
Or siren glances which contain
The ravishment and social bane
　For carnal youth of giddy head ;

So is the ball-room of the gay
　To *debutantes* in *la beau-monde*.
When peaceful night is changed to day
And Sensuality has play
　Of passions in their fitful round.

LXXXIII.

I catch a glimpse of passing show;
    I see a throng décolleté;
And by the grand parade I know
Terpsichore doth rule below,
    And these are signs of her rapt sway.

The flush of youth dyes cheek and brow,
    And aided has the hand of art;
Soft eyes here blaze as though somehow
Their liquid depths caught fire and now
    Give light to show their passion's heart:

And robbed the rainbow is of hues
    To drape these butterflies of Night;
And naught resplendant doth refuse
To add a luster for the use
    Of Beauty in her brilliant dight!

LXXXIV.

The gayest of the gay are here;
    The simple in their giddy plight;
The shallowest of the sham appear
Commingling with the brilliant near,
    And liberty doth give delight!

Eyes promise much and preasures more,
    And languidness entices love;
The pulsing heart now quickens flow
Of passion but to crimson snow
    Of bosoms throbbing dreams of love:

And then, as vines entwined, they wind
    Their satyr-sylph-like arms around,
As tendrils so to hold and bind
In union here these polar kind,
    Magnetic by the touch and sound!

And, drunk with passion's melody,
    They move with love's voluptuousness,
And swell with billows of the sea
That rolls within in mutiny
    To wiser thoughts of soberness!

They glide as things unreal, insooth,
    Like wild Gyrini on a pool;
They reel and skirt in very truth
Like lambs agambol full of youth,
    Or madcaps on the eve of Yule.

LXXXV.

If waltz delight you, whirl ye on :
    The scene will change to find you low
Of all the plain ye stood upon
Irradiant when your life begun—
    And ye will never find it more!

Youth will be past and blushes gone—
    No rouge to bring them back to life!
And honor will be trampled on,
And virtue of its merit shorn
    By midnight revels and love's strife!

And barriers down which held apart
　　Wild passions that should feel restraint,
Will open way to lustful heart
For lecherous charm to play its part
　　And leave the soul a lasting taint!

LXXXVI.

The Dervish has his day and falls:
　　Ye with your dance of less excuse,
Arouse a nature that recalls
The social curse—though such befalls
　　One sex alone in its abuse!

Man's jealousy doth urge on man
　　The purity of wife and maid;
For what is chaste he lays his plan,
And to obtain her so he can
　　By spurning here the fallen jade.

He states his wants; he makes demand,
　　And, howsoever low himself,
His manhood still will firmly stand
And call for virtue though he plann'd
　　The downfall of the sex itself!

But woman on her part doth yield
　　To question not what she receives!
And this is her great moral wield!
And this is how her virtues shield!
　　She falls but seldom self retrieves!

LXXXVII.

Her innate wish may be as wild
　　As any act that man can do;
Her moral nature undefiled
Because by custom she's the child
　　Of man's selection and his rue.

She has no scruples as the man
　　In the selection of her mate;
If she but love the flame she'll fan
Although it be for vilest man
　　Found in the most degraded state!

LXXXVIII.

To thus contrast the sexes we
　　See much that seems not just or right;
The man inordinately free,
The woman lost to all if she
　　But once embrace a social blight:

And yet the man can soon forget;
　　For all the world is his engross:
While woman in her sphere must fret
And suffer martyrdom, and yet
　　Be comfort to some man, of course!

The fault is Nature's, but the creed
　　Is writ in language as divine
As oracle which places deed
Of patience far above the seed
　　Of man that evils here incline.

LXXXIX.

A woman's love or hate is spring
 That moves her hands to any deed ;
In love her heart defies the fling,
Or Fate's or Fortune's sharpest sting :
 She hides her wounds to let them bleed!

A creature of divinest love
 Whose soul with fondness overflows,
And sympathy of God above
Stands not superior, nor His love,
 Than glows the spark her bosom knows :

A patient grace of tenderness ;
 A witch of passion that's divine ;
A nurse to all the ills that press ;
A cherub of sweet blessedness
 Consoling all who may repine :

She glides an angel on this earth ;
 She stands for that faith would proclaim ;
She gives to blessing lives their birth,
So proving mother of all worth
 And sweet almoner of love's aim.

XC.

But woman's hate is that degree
 Of hell as that her love is bliss!
When scorned, neglected, then can she
Unburden spleen and so set free
 The rancor of a Nemesis!

Hell holds no depth she can't explore
    To fetch an ill to torture life;
Medusa-like her hate would glow
To murder in its glance and show
    The venom of her nature's strife.

She conjures ill and heaps her scorn
    With spirit that a Harpy loved;
She'll give a Judas kiss and fawn,
And e'en her sacred honor pawn
    To hide the vixen in her moved!

XCI.

But why expatiate on this?
    Why contrast man's or woman's wiles?
Why pry to wreck our little bliss
By proving natures are remiss
    In all except their selfish guiles?

Is earth not full enougn of woe?
    Are hearts too free, or spirits light?
Are dreams at fault because we know
Ephem'ral is the feeble glow
    That lights a hope to mundane sight?

Return to nature; gaze around:
    Mark her vicissitudes and moods.
Forget the fetters that are wound
Confining us upon the ground
    As prey entangled in the woods:

That Soul is free which yet can soar
   In fancy realms though body lies
In dungeons cold and bare; and more,
That Soul is free which tunes the roar
   Of Death to anthems of the skies!

XCII.

I feel a humid breath of air;
   I see a slumberous, lazy, haze;
I note the heaven's darkening care,
And thistledown on languorous air
   Come floating in the sultry rays;

I hear the droning of a bee
   That drifts upon the swelling wind;
I catch a muffled song of glee
That bursts from throats I can not see,
   And birds hie to their fellow-kind;

I catch a bay from yonder wold
   That tells a tale of sore distress,
And bleats and bellows from some fold
Are lowly sounds which speak the scold
   Of higher Powers that repress:

The perfumes of some ladened bloom
   Make rendolent the drowsy air:
Alack! the scene is one of gloom:
The sounds are knellings of the doom
   That comes engulfing here the fair!

XCIII.

The strato-mist we called a haze
Has swelled to cumuli of storm,
And all the heavens are ablaze
With flashes of the lightning's rays
That zigzag in their anger's form :

Like demons roused to wrath and hate,
Fire Jötuns leap from cloud to cloud,
And play as though aërial state
Was home of some wild, wrathful, Fate
That grinned to give the earth its shroud!

Or Gnomes that snatch at fleeting prey
And such pursue : so seem the arms
Flashed from dark folds; each grasping ray
More fearful by its scorching play
That spreads to strike e'en while it charms!

And presently there comes the roar
Of Winds let loose to howl apace :
They drive the raging Storm before
To wreck as some base living foe
That glories in a wanton chase .

And thunder is the chuckling laugh
Of this old demon we call Storm!
The flash his smile, the rod his staff,
The Winds his charges; the riffraff
Of formless things tell of his harm!

No reins of Æolus can hold
  The furies of the tempest's sweep;
He may as well return to fold
Whence issued forces uncontrolled,
  Though ancients locked them in his keep.

XCIV.

O Demons of the stormy sky,
  What god-womb of the world can hold
Each thundering Shade or Deity
That stands the symbol of the sigh
  The Tempest heaves when full of scold?

Can Greek or Roman Pantheon,
  Or wilder Æsir of the north,
Or Deva where the gods begun,
Ahura of the burning sun,
  Tell whence or when the Storm comes forth?

I see in tempests Thor of old;
  I see in lightnings mjolnir hurl'd;
The crashing is his stride so bold;
The howling winds his wrathful scold;
  His frown the darkness of the world!

I see a Hoder in the Gloom
  The wrath of mighty Thor pursues;
But Baldur soon will re-illume,
When, resurrected from the tomb,
  He comes in all his vernal hues!

I see a Zeus; a Jupiter;
   A Ra of strange ethereal fire;
An Indra of the Hindu seer;
Jehovah of the Hebrew fear,—
   All gods of Storm and Heaven's ire!

Which one is God of all the rest
   And shadowed in the others' glow?
Which one controls, and which is best,
Or which can better stand the test
   Of reason here, I do not know.

I only know that nations have—
   Each in its own peculiar way—
Defined their gods and counted slave
Him who believed in other save
   Their own *wise* superstition's sway!

And so I turn my eyes about
   To see them all, and reason why
Analogy, to help me out,
Turns all into a frenzied shout,
   Their protestations much awry.

And thus but for the poet's dream,
   Which made each wild conception fair,
We would acknowledge it a theme
Of barbarism, or the scheme
   Of the more blatant man of care.

And sacred Eddas of the Nord,
  Or Sagas we once thought divine,
Are just as much in truth's accord
As Oriental tales of fraud
  That give us now a faith and shrine.

XCV.

Akin religious faith; akin
  Desires which have brought them forth;
Akin the passions that have been;
Akin the human race to sin
  And every broken trust or oath:

Akin each age to that before,
  And that decadence bids welcome;
Akin the social states below,
The brute to man, the high and low;
  Each thing that calls this earth a home!

Our vanity may close our eyes,
  Our egotism may control;
But Truth will see the linking ties,
And how we magnify our size
  And claim a god-like, lofty, soul!

I've seen man groping in the dark;
  I've seen him lost in grim despair;
I've seen him full of fear to hark
And catch an omen from the lark,
  Or harmless leapings of the hare!

Or radiance he sees in flame
  That is his own *auto-da-fa;*
And by some martyrdom proclaim
Reward hereafter and the fame
  That lives with fools from day to day!

XCVI.

Yea, like are we in barbarous deeds
  To bestial ancestors we scorn;
We loudly vaunt our senseless creeds,
And credit claim where it were needs
  We blush for thoughts so lowly born!

Our highest faiths are but the sum
  Of totem dreams the savage knew;
We give hallucinations home
And coddle every vagrant tome
  That idly speaks of heaven's due.

The god of Wish our fathers knew,
  When Norsemen they of simple faith,
Is yet the god of much we do,
The impulse that would here renew
  The little hope which wisdom hath:

And to that god we bow and say,
  'Since Reason here is blind or dumb,
We thank thee for the fatuous ray
Thou givest us to light the way
  For Guess to see beyond the tomb!'

XCVII.

The total of life's subtilties
  Is not the sum of any faith :
Within them all some frenzy tries
To paint more brilliantly hope's skies
  To please the fancy of earth's wraith!

And when men's faiths dispute and war,
  It is the strife of fools, withal ;
'Tis bigotry that brings the jar
To social peace and helps debar
  Love's scheme of brotherhood to all.

Arbitrament of war is death
  Death to the faiths that stir the strife ;
Death to the soul's diviner breath
That wakes the hopes within, and death
  To dreams which would enchant this life.

Stir man to see the little light
  A faith can cast and he will scorn
Its feeble ray and find delight
In setting all the world aright,
  Though disenchantment so is born :

A disenchantment that will blight
  Our hopes in dreams of things to be ;
Philosophy the only light
To guide us through the starless Night
  That falls when Faith can no more see!

Yet still each tongue should tell the truth
  Though hope be lost and faith denied :
What profits man to hide the ruth
That some experience will, forsooth,
  Bring on us in our pomp of pride?

Whatever mysticism may
  Our judgment for awhile confuse,
A reason will arise some day,—
If we'll but give our thoughts fair play,—
  And proneing minds will disabuse.

XCVIII.

A faith in after-death depends
  On vainer selfishness in man
Who cries his own exalted ends ;
But naught below him thither tends—
  If egotism holds the plan !

The subtleties he brings to bear
  To prove divinity of life,
Are in behalf of his own care ;
The rest are all denied a share
  In things immortal—though of strife !

Yet, if analogy be true,
  The least that lives is as divine
As any Spark that ever blew
In soul of him whose wisdom knew
  The right from wrong as they entwine !

XCIX.

The vastness of the world is awe
  To man or brute of finite mind;
We're seeking ever after Law,
But learn not that expression's flaw
  Is in the words which have defined.

The bigot says that man alone
  Has consciousness and eye of truth;
And yet how know we that our scorn
Hides not a due more lowly born—
  A due we owe the brute, insooth?

Our moral sense is born of fear;
  Of fear and profit got of peace:
We shoulder social state of care,
To let our selfishness compare
  The burden with the ill's increase,

And, finding more of ill than good,
  We lay it to some Deity:
Our own shortcomings then we hood
To wash with faith's " vicarious blood "
  And claim "elected purity "!

C.

O Vanity that would aspire
  To Homes celestial but debar
Thy fellows from " ethereal fire "
Because by nature their desire
  Is speechless at the earthly bar!

Who knows but what the Spirit moves
　　As much in acorns as in men?
And that the throbbing Forest proves
Some Animation that behooves
　　A patient mercy there again?

Humanity, thou framest laws;
　　But be thou governed by the tie
Of Sentiency! Plead thou the cause
Of mercy ere some Life doth pause,
　　Through man's abuse, to sink and die!

Bless, too, the creed that sees a soul
　　In tree or flower, beast or bird;
That lets an angel's touch control
The impulse of a savage soul
　　Which laughs to give Destruction word:

For Pantheism is divine!
　　What fairer God evolved by thought
Stands symbol for a brighter shrine
Than that all things etern combine
　　To leave us happiness so wrought?

CI.

Who has not seen a summer's dawn
　　Where peaks and clouds were tinged with red;
Where light, like scimeter out-drawn,
Sharp cleaved the Night, so ghastly wan,
　　To splash its blood on skies o'erhead,

The blood to spread as blush of day
  So bidding welcome to the Sun?
So comes the light of Truth : so may
A Genius rise with shooting ray
  To light the gloom Fear feeds upon!

The rose of Fancy coyly blushed
  Its richness in the brain of man,
And fertile Imagery was flushed,
And wild Invention, soaring, hushed,
  When Genius came the world to scan.

When Genius came the world to scan
  It saw a Homer lost in lore,
It saw a Shakespeare in the man,
It saw a Milton's range and span ;
  It gave their souls impulse to soar ;

To sweep the earth and skies of truth
  To crystalize in gems of thought ;
To seize the world's departing youth,
Transfix its beauty and its blowth
  And chain the image Time had wrought!

It taught a Pindar, nursed a Burns
  To sing the psalms of pain and toil ;
It woke a Dante's soul with yearns
For Paradise and love that spurns
  The doubt that hangs on Faith's recoil ;

It so enriched the hampered mind
    Imagination leaped to see
The beauties that were undefined
Though all around it here consigned,
    Awaiting Genius to be free!

CII.

When Genius came upon the world
    It met a cold reception there :
It found the human heart was churl'd,
And low all aspirations hurl'd
    By mundane mockery and despair :

It found a barren field for work ;
    Cocagne of brag for Paradise!
A mental caliber to shirk ;
A spirit more depraved to lurk,
    Bethwarting all that Honor tries !

It eked its day 'mid toil and pain ;
    It labored for its visioned goal ;
With patience gathered little gain,
And for that bore the brunt and bain—
    The stigma of a witless soul!

Too deep for fellowship, at first
    Poor Genius was pronounced a fool !
But shackles of the mind it burst
And lit the gloom of things accurst.
    And gave each wandering thought a rule.

Its force creative stirred, withal;
   A Titan was within the strife:
Volition leaped to duty's call—
Olympian heights could ne'er appall
   The impulse born of such a life!

The future pays the homage due
   The heroes of the scornful past;
And Fame, though laggard with the new,
Adorns the dead, and hides from view
   The rancor that could never last.

CIII.

On wings we soar when thoughts have sway
   Untrammeled by terrestrial bounds,
And phantom creatures people day,
And thoughts delight in elfish play
   When Fancy plodding Fact confounds:

For slumbering in the soul is spark
   Of wild, unmanumitted, thought;
Strike fetters off, and, like a lark,
It soars aloft describing mark
   Of that ethereal Forces wrought!

And thus was fashioned man's delight;
   And from this source sprung songs of love;
And many visions thus had flight
To blush the nadir of the Night
   And trace a mock-dawn high above!

CIV.

The Kalpa of a world it sees;
   Annihilation in its end :
An Avatar of blissful ease
Wherein a Vishnu comes to please
   And human strife with love to blend;

Or threshold of Elysium
   And naught but peace forevermore;
Or dawn of Hope's Millennium
With rest of all that's wearisome,
   Or what may start a thought of woe!

It matters not the faith or creed,
   Nor what we call the goal and end;
Each Age and Nation knows God's deed,
And claims as true alone its creed—
   The rest to wild delusion tend!

And Wisdom labors still in vain
   To open minds locked in conceit;
And though the world has borne the stain
Of warring faiths upon its plain,
   No sect as yet will own defeat!

For man is ever vain to boast
   A truth beyond his mental grasp;
And when in deepest mystery lost
And thought in chaos truly tost,
   He claims to see Delusion's clasp!

And so we pass from stage to stage
  Reviewing Life's vain earthly span ;
Now marveling at the wit's engage,
Now laughing at the antic wage
  That marks the pageantry of man.

CV.

The fairest of the flowers grown
  In soil of man's existence here,
Is Truth, and though but feebly blown,
Its perfume is the richest known
  In making sweet the social sphere.

A tonic of the soul its balm
  Can heal the wound a lie has rent,
Soothe Conscience of its aching qualm,
And bring to troubled thoughts a calm
  Divine within its sweet content.

And wheresoever throned is Truth
  There is the shrine of all that's good ;
And there may Virtue live in youth
Though seeing cumbent head of Ruth
  Bowed to its rosary and rood !

CVI.

The hills are brown ; the trees show stains
  Of gold and red 'mid fading green ;
The furrowed fields for winter grains
Stretch faraway o'er searing mains,
  And lonely is the passing scene.

The sky is clear and calm and blue,
  And silence reigns within the day;
And all around the brilliant hue
Of dying Summer meets the view—
  The blush of verdure in decay.

We know by drifting leaves and sighs
  That sunny hours of joy are few;
We know by opalescent skies
And russet woods, that Nature dies
  To pay the rolling Seasons' due:

And now to Winter's ruthless care
  The subtle charms of Summer hie;
And trees to biting winds will bare
Their trunks to stand grim spectres there—
  Bleak monuments to parts that die.

CVII.

Autumnal days, Autumnal days,
  What sadness in your fleeting scene!
What visions float within the haze
That comes with earth's departing rays,
  The fading glow of summer's sheen?

Yea, like a funeral pyre of life,
  A blaze of glory is your death;
And all decadence here is rife
With sad remembrance of the strife
  Harassing everything of breath.

The winds cry through your drooping boughs
  'Stho' wailing death of all that's good ;
While petals of frost-faded flowers,
And fronds of seed, in drifting showers,
  Are scattered in the fields and wood :

And in the dying year we see
  The symbol of Life's fleeting span ;
We see the Great stript as the tree,
And, reft of honor, left to be
  The simulacrum of the Man !

We see the goal of Faith and Hope
  Fall from its sceptred throne on high ;
We see proud Grandeur's downward slope,
The narrow range of all its scope
  Wherein to live and fight and die ;

And seeing this we know how vain
  Is man to boast his might or worth ;
For in Time's reckoning it is plain
His glory cannot long remain
  For exultation on this earth.

CVIII.

In scenes like these what truths arise
  Awakening dreams to thoughts profound?
Proud man may face with true surprise
The shifting of each fellow's guise—
  Which brings all heads low to the ground !

The Carpo season of the world
  When man should gather harvests in :—
Hast thou so garnered up each pearl
Of wisdom? or been dunce or churl
  To fill thy coffers full of sin?

Thy day of need draws now apace :
  Need of the riches fled and gone!
Need of the happiness we chase
In childhood's blissful hour, or trace
  In benisons the man hath known!

The dole of Spring and Summer flies;
  'Tis Autumn brings us thought's regret :
A buoyant heart 'neath brilliant skies
In gloomy weather often dies,
  If other moods bid it forget;

Forget that future days may want
  The things so lavish to the youth,
When Plenty pines till lean and gaunt
The seasons find the man, his vaunt
  The mock of senile hope and truth!

CIX.

And yet these Autumn days that bring
  Sad memories of pleasures past,
Or show us faults that left their sting,
Can also give us thoughts of Spring,
  Reanimating all at last!

Earth dies, but Death is only sleep,
  And, Baldur like, it wakes again
To bring us joy, and, while we weep
Its death, old Time doth slowly creep
  To bring us Life, sunshine and rain ;

Sunshine and rain to quicken Life
  And hurry pleasures to their place ;
To stir the nascent germ of strife ;
To bud the fields with blossoms rife
  With all the hues the rainbows trace :

For, Winter past, the earth again
  Blooms forth in beauty and in cheer ;
And, what in gloom has fearful been,
May prove a good with power to win
  The soul from its low groveling care.

So may it be with all ; and when
  Senescent grown, may newer Light
Illume the sky and once again
Reanimate the Soul and then
  Bid morning to the chill of Night !

CX.

Farewell ye passing days of joy !
  Farewell ye seasons full of youth !
Farewell, but let our hopes employ
Your visions left recalling joy
  To spirits darkened by the truth :

Farewell! we wait the advent here
　　Of Springtime with its skies of blue;
And, 'round the fire-side's glowing cheer,
We'll sit and dream while seasons drear
　　Creep on to all the world renew :

We'll wait and while we eke the hour
　　We'll talk of moments once enjoyed ;
And through imagination's power
That colors thought's mysterious flower,
　　We'll live as though again employed.

Most of our pleasures are in dreams,
　　And absence stills each aching pain ;
Aloof, the past a heaven seems
So full the glow of mellowed beams
　　That fall entrancing Manhood's wane.

Most of our ills imagined, too,
　　Or self-inflicted without cause ;
The grusomeness of thoughts to do
The ill that ages long may rue
　　Unconscious of these sequent laws.

So Wisdom would the chalice fling,
　　All brimming with its poisoned draught,
Into the Past to let the sting
Left from its bitter contents bring
　　The thoughts of other potions quaft.

CXI.

Then fill the empty bowl of cheer !
   Heap fagots on the smouldering fire!
We'll toast and drink to seasons drear,
The bumpers sparkling ruby tear
   Shed by old Summer to expire!

Around the hearth-stone of our home
   We'll talk of days of joy and pain ;
We'll talk of times when weary roam
Oppressed each wanderer without home
   Or social comfort in his plane ;

We'll watch the silhouetted dreams
   Traced by the fire's soft flickering light ;
Deciphering faces in the beams
Instinct with life : for truly seems
   This fancy to the mind to-night.

We're young again and springtide stirs
   The first impulse of youth, and Love
Is raptuous with each hope that purrs
To wish, and to the heart recurs
   The image of departed Love !

Too soon the soot mars fairness seen,
   And we have blackened embers there
Of Fancy's dream ! A truth, I ween,
That lacks not vision that is keen
   To pierce hallucinations fair !

For when the flames in ashes lie
  The dream they shadowed forth is sped;
The wish that gave it birth to die
And leave the bosom with its sigh
  That interest in it all is dead.

And interest is the zest of life,
  The spice that seasons things, which, when
We lose, it leaves us but the strife
And eking of a dreary life
  In routine of itself again.   .

CXII.

The dream dispelled, we see the fact
  That rudely hurls our idols down:
Life is a season's strange compact
'Tween Growth and stern Decay; an act
  Omnific with a fatal crown!

Each season is a symbol, too,
  That marks the different stages here:
In Spring and Summer Force is new
And full of energy to do
  The part that wish may hold as dear;

In Autumn powers weaken fast
  And shed their bloom for ripened thought;
In Winter comes the leadened cast
When thoughts would linger in the past
  And hoard what memory has caught:

'Tis then the May-day's song and sky,
    And Youth and Love 'neath basking sun,
And Autumn with its rich supply,
December's want, hoar Age's cry,
    Are in our dreams compounded one :

'Tis then the virtuous acts of youth
    Know their reward's vitality ;
'Tis then man feels the strength of truth,
The throb and sting of folly's ruth
    If life was passed in vanity.

The Ages are as Life. each one
    An epoch is of good or bad ;
A day of silly quib and pun
Where folly is the rule, or one
    Wherein the senses are not mad :

Each leaves its mark to coming years :
    The eon of the dunce to pass
Degenerating hopes and fears ;
The age of Virtue into years
    Bright with the deeds that merit has.

CXIII.

Belike this age unto the first
    In which some folly was the rule ;
For true the world is foully curst
With pompous Vanity, and, worst
    Of all, the ignorance of the fool !

We magnify our little wits
   And think the dupe's diversions wise;
We mumble Folly's choice tidbits
And move to sentimental fits,
   And claim a knowledge by surmise!

A paresis has come, indeed,
   To mark this vaunted age of man!
Degenerate his social creed,
And lower still the thought and deed
   Now circumscribed by Fashion's span!

So, with the passing of the year,
   We mark decadence of the race:
Each manly attribute is queer:
The woman takes the leading share—
   To run the world with powdered face!

A spasm of rare sentiment
   For what is called a " bondage " here,
Has led the age to wild intent
That time will show irrelevant
   To object of a woman's care.

If she indeed lacks liberty,
   'Tis by her nature, not through man:
She is a slave to Fashion's plea;
The dupe of vain Frivolity;
   The coquette of a fad and fan!

First let her free herself and then
    Lend helping hand for her advance
A mind so narrowed in its ken
That show is all supreme, again
    Must strive for freedom's arm and lance.

CXIV.

Her present stride marks man's decay,
    And not her own advancement here ;
Effeminate he is to-day,
And social fallacies betray
    Conditions that the wise may fear.

He calls surrender ' chivalry ' !
    Surrender of his rank in life !
Surrender of virility
For cozened smile Viginity
    May cast him for his sensual strife !

The " age of chivalry " must stand
    The commentation of the fool ;
Not that a courtesy is bann'd,
But that a tournament is plann'd
    By cockneys of a woman's rule.

We call " Dark Age " of history
    The time man was the woman's slave ;
When " Knighthood " was the vanity,
And strife for plume or glove, decree
    Of Honor with the dolt and knave !

Cervantes is not but the day
    For his return is drawing nigh;
The clamor is for marshal play;
Reward is in a smile or lay
    To gallantry that is awry!

CXV.

O modesty, O modesty,
    Where art thou flown in this mad chase
Of brazen woman who would ply
Her arts to help her to decry
    Distinction in the sex and race?

Attired as man she apes his ways
    And claims a right to thwart the end
Of nature, and, in her wild craze,
To social functions gives a phase
    That naught of virtue can commend.

The comely creature of our dream—
    Which Romance loves to weave in tale—
Is but a barren thought, 'twould seem,
Throbbed to beguile the troubled stream
    Of life, or hush love's piteous wail.

The bifurcated creature now
    Despises all and is despised;
Her way the world will sure allow, -
But man will make with her no vow
    In that she lacks all he has prized.

CXVI.

In literature the woman rules!
　　Ideas of the man are low;
He wanders after certain " schools ";
He mystifies himself and pules
　　Like any child for passing show!

For 'schools' of imbecility
　　Where want of thought is merit shown:
The writer of this day must sigh,
Ejaculate, and show how nigh
　　To simper madness he is grown!

Must deal in some uncouth conceit,
　　And drivel in his metaphors;
Must prove his weary thoughts effete,—
And commentation is complete
　　When critic praise rewards his course!

CXVII.

A maudlin age has come upon
　　Us in this evil hour of grace;
Around the things which we should shun
Is hung the halo duty won,
　　And Sin presents a smiling face!

For woman sways the world; her grief
　　She cries o'er judgment of the law;
And for a brute she prays relief;
Strews flowers in his path as if
　　The road of dalliance that he saw

Was God's device to lead him in
    And so accomplish end divine!—
The will of God can be no sin!—
A Paradise that brute will win
    Although atrocious deeds combine

'Mong brutes to make this world a hell
    More dreadful by His helpful hand!
And so by woman's gentle spell,
We must to justice say farewell
    And let the foolish take command!

CXVIII.

" 'Tis better ninety-nine be lost
    Than one be left alone in sin!"
And this is what the fable cost
That told of prodigal once lost
    But to return to fold again

For great rejoicing and love-feast
    Of " Fatted Calf," and honor's place!
Reward for being once a beast
Prone to the wallow and the yeast
    Of passions that alone debase!

" Each youth has sometime ' wild oats' sown,
    And each must feel a ' whirl-wind's ' breath;
For by iniquity is shown,
In contrast, God's care for his own,
    And woeful end of Sin and Death!"

A fable sounding well, 'tis true,
  But lacking wisdom and foresight;
For should the world once turn to do
As such would teach, it would renew
  The ages loathed as Reason's night.

CXIX.

The sowing of " wild oats " is done
  When Life is withered to old age;
And harvest of the " whirl-wind's " fun
Is a perennial, lasting one,
  Recorded in each day and page!

The youth by some wild passion tost
  May be reclaimed, but he is one
To thousands in their folly lost;
And reformations often cost
  The worth of what an hundred won!

Sin as a hero can not pose
  Without results we must deplore;
And pleasures once begot of woes
Will find some relic of the throes
  Remaining but to prick the sore:

For nature takes account of all:
  You can not pay her with a word!
She holds the debtor for his fall;
She gives inheritance the gall
  Bequeathed of ills we thought deferred!

CXX.

But yet this is the trend of thought—
  Of modern thought effete and vain!
And he who is not frenzy fraught
By luring sighs, is deemed as naught,
  Or brute or madman to refrain!

A thing of mystery and scorn;
  A creature wanting heart and soul;
Misogynist of woman's warn,
Because he does not fondle, fawn,
  And give the petticoat control!

'Mid fawning life alone he seems
  Because with thoughts more lonely still;
He finds that pleasures all are dreams,
And that the mind with visions teems
  When that it entertains the will.

Poor man to cherish no conceit—
  For wantonness doth still disguise!
How rude unto thyself to treat
The heart in its love-wakened beat
  For what it profits to be wise!

CXXI.

I fear he can not love, and why?
  Not that he lacks the sentiment,
Nor passion born of lust, nor sigh
Of fellowship, nor wish to cry
  The need of any soul's content,

Nor eye for beauty, nor the heart
   That holds in solace thoughts devout,
Nor brain for artifice or art,
Nor any impulse for the part
   Of fancy nor in pleasure's bout;

Not these, but that he hath an eye
   Which selfish secrets would discern;
A spirit that would lust defy
And stifle in the throat the lie
   That here would spring to do Love's turn.

Man loves when selfishness doth reign;
   He hates when broken is its rule;
He fears when knowledge would explain
The trend of passions, how they train
   The will to make it folly's tool.

Love is of Lust, and Lust of Life,
   And Life is spark through this desire;
It is a chain linked here in strife,
And every forging still is rife
   With evils of the natal fire!

How low soever sprung that germ,
   It kindred bears to all the past;
And, though exalted, still a worm
Which stings and bites an earthly term,
   To wiggle back to dust at last!

Survival in life's battle here
　Has higher aim or lower mark
As rules the intellect, or fear,
Or wantonness, or driveling care,
　Or lightest humor of the lark.

CXXII.

We'll not admit that Love is Lust,
　Desire on which the race depends,
And yet once give the passions trust
And all restraints too soon will burst
　To bare the heart to vicious ends;

To bare the heart and leave it prone
　To mischief and its nameless deeds;
The light we thought within us shone,
So smothered in its sensual zone
　It throws no ray on senseless creeds!

'Tis thus the closets still must bear
　The skeletons of much professed;
And virtue, which man doth declare
Is due to faith, finds little care
　When faith is guide alone or test!

CXXIII.

Move on, O Time, we can not stay
　The wheels of cycles slipping by!
Each moment is a cam, each day
A splicing felloe on the way
　To circuit of Eternity!

Each change escapement of the flow
  Recorded on the dial Earth;
Each phase decree for Life to show
Its adaptation here to grow
  And fix itself for future birth.

Before inventive brain or hand
  Caught at thy fleeting images,
Thou hadst the power to command
And stamp thy changes on the land
  And sea, in heaven's prodigies.

A god to ancients, yet to man
  A fate that knows no sympathy;
Thou breakest up his boasted plan
And measurest off his little span
  To give him Death's infinity!

Thou bringest labors which are vain;
  Thou settest him in divers ways;
He hopes some knowledge here to gain,
But moves at tangent by the strain
  Of thy recurring change and phase!

He strives and struggles and would give
  Life's energies in hopes to know
The secret of Want's suppletive—
And when he has but learned to live,
  Death comes to bid him rise and go!

O Time, thou abstract chain of woes!
    Thou link of blisses forged to God!
Thou " fleeting image " of the pose
Eternity a moment shows
    To change with swiftness of a nod!

For Father Chronos still devours
    The offspring of his gat to-day:
The earth and sea and Being's powers,
The sun's fair rays, the blushing flowers,
    And everything of breath and clay!

CXXIV.

From Youth to Age and Age to Death,
    Man would each life hold in review;
Would trace each struggling thing of breath,
Count throbs from birth to pain of death,
    And wonders note in passing through:

He would the purpose and the end,
    And so the final Destiny;
And what repays one to contend,
And what reward when actions trend
    To ethics of philosophy;

Philosophy of wisdom born,
    Not cant of Epicurean brew;
Nor cult of sterner Stoic's scorn;
Nor any special ssytem's spawn;
    But all compounded in the new:

The broad idea of the man
   Begot of all the ages gone ;
Whose judgment, with its greater span,
The future may the better plan
   And blaze the way that leads us on.

To such an eye the scene is one
   Of fleckered lights and shades of strife,
Predominating now the Sun
With gladsome light of duty done,
   And then the Shadows of each life ;

Unfolding so a tale of woe
   That hangs upon a feeble breath,
Yet blasting hopes of fortunes glow,
And making of this life a bore
   That ends but in the gasps of Death !

But if man's wisdom can not see
   Beyond this wild, abysmal, gloom ;
If all his hopes of bliss to be
Are lost in wise Philosophy,
   Why shudder at a fancied doom ?

'Twere better in the peaceful state
   Oblivion promises to all,
Than all this rancor and debate
Aroused to tell the tale of fate
   That none can alter or forestall.

CXXV.

Life, Death, and the Hereafter, men
　　Come prating of as though they knew
Aught of God's purpose, how or when
He moves or wills, or, even then,
　　What He has set for us to do.

They would prescribe their Deity
　　And set a limit to His will!
He who professes here an eye
That sees into the future, why,
　　He little knows his feeble skill!

The utmost that each one can learn
　　Is that he simply nothing knows,
Save that to him the world is stern,
And labors rise at every turn
　　Harassing Life unto its close.

CXXVI.

We know that we know nothing, yet
　　The world is full of pedantry
That wisely looks and nods to let
True wisdom see its worth and get
　　A plumbing of mentality!

We know that we know nothing, then
　　Why here profess an eye, or mind,
That sees, or comprehends God when
The knowledge in itself would then
　　Prove us but stumbling creatures blind?

Or if we know God's wish or word,
    Why all these divers faiths and ways?
Are warring tenets here absurd
To give the Devil all the herd
    Of wild fanatics of each craze?

CXXVII.

We know that we know nothing, but
    We grasp at things intangible,
And blindly fall into the rut
Of Ignorance that's worn and cut
    By folly indefensible.

We here conjecture, or we guess,
    And trust ourselves to be deceived;
We get our thoughts into a mess
And horror minds with some distress
    'Twere foolish, sure, to be believed!

The lesson Time would teach us all
    Is that we only half can see;
And that the story of " Man's Fall,"
In such half-light, is fable all,
    As well as knowing what's to be.

CXXVIII.

Believe or not, man's faith is shorn
    Of much that lent a pleasing ray;
We must confess that place and bourne
Of Death's dark Province is unknown,
    And blank the speech of fanes each day.

Faith is not here advanced by sight,
  Nor foresight cleared by help of Faith;
The coming of the mental light
Estrange the two, and each with might
  Assails the other's fading wraith!

'Tis hard to bring ourselves to say
  The " light " we thought we saw in youth
Was but a feeble, flickering ray
Of egotism : when its day
  Is past comes advent of the Truth!

Though knowledge gives us wider range
  For play of all the intellect,
The mind is rid of creatures strange,
And Faith can never more arrange
  Incongruous thoughts to such aspect.

Each age has martyred someone who
  Denied the faith that ruled his day;
And each accusor found his rue,
And Bigotry that rose and slew,
  Lived to behold its own dismay!

CXXIX.

Like flights of strange, migrating birds,
  Or shadows chasing flying clouds,
We meet in wild, stampeding, herds,
To mingle, pass, or greet with words
  Unheard, or lost within the crowds;

IN PASSING THROUGH.

We meet within a narrow span,
  We glance into a kindly face;
We feel a kindredship in man;
We seek a comrade there who can
  Help us to eke the time and place:

We meet and dream a sweet conceit;
  We find an object then to love;
But ere that dream is yet complete,
Some babbling fact will sure defeat
  The end—and in the Night we move!

We meet and pass and scarcely know
  What thing did disenchant our dream;
The dullness of the after-glow
We feel, but find the light no more,
  And see alone a fancied beam!

Love is the child of youthful days,
  The sweet companion of old age;
Consoling in its willful ways,
Tormenting if the truth portrays
  The just demerit of its rage.

The light we saw in passing eye
  Was but desire within our own;
Reflection's cast too soon to die
And leave us but the wistful sigh
  That comes to tell us hope is flown!

CXXX.

We meet in highways of this life,
  We nod and pass and then forget;
Our thoughts insistent on the strife
We wage for station, rank and life :
  And so it simply stands, ' we met ' !

'Twere better we should meet and part
  And strangers so continue still,
Than that we should awake a heart
To feel the keen and bitter smart
  That comes with knowledge of its ill.

The dream might stir a latent flame
  That best were left in slumber deep ;
And passion might arouse to claim
A mastery and bring to shame
  The spirit of our restful sleep.

Adieu, we say, and kiss our hand,
  Departing on our several ways :
We thus retain our heart's command
And wisely see and understand
  The danger of a passing craze !

CXXXI.

And so we journey on to age
  And winter of the dying year ;
Recording hope and joy and rage
And pain and death on every page
  The Book of Life doth open here.

A strange fatality it seems
   Attends us on our lowly way;
Lives frothing like fierce mountain streams
That leap wild cataracts—for beams,
   Of light to flash the rainbow's ray!

But Dawn or Eve hath rainbow-ray,
   And not the Noon-tide's burning light;
The first forewarning for the day,
The other promise that we may
   See less of Storm within the Night!

They both betokening broken skies
   That sift the sunshine of a hope;
They speak of balmy seasons, dyes
Of spring, and not the winter skies
   Which lower heaven's gloomy scope.

CXXXII.

In summing up the deeds of earth
   We find more ills withal than bliss;
Conflicting from the hour of birth
Are all the acts we deem of worth,
   And none of them gives happiness!

A serpent coils within the nest
   Of happy bird that buildeth low;
And lowly mortals seeking rest
May find a dungeon as their quest,
   And peace but pain forevermore!

All greatness is of little worth,
  Tho' magnified to worldly eyes,
And equal is the lowest birth
To the most lordly one of earth,
  For each is leveled when he dies!

No artifice can Time convince,
  Nor trick devise a happiness;
The old, the young, or pauper, prince,
All in some earthly stock must wince,
  And here endure some painful stress.

Who finds contentment gropes it blind,
  Is proverb learned too late in life;
And strength is wasted in the wind
Of thought and deed we give to find
  A way avoiding earthly strife.

No happiness, no earthly bliss
  Awarding pains or sorrows borne;
As light as silly Fancy's kiss
Is the caress of Happiness,
  And we arouse to find it gone!

To find it gone and in its place
  The void of utter loneliness;
Sweet memory alone to trace
The cherished hope, the wily grace,
  That contrast here this evil press!

No happiness! no happiness!
  I've reached the point where Envy cries
For lot of others, yea, in stress
Of anything that holds caress
  For simple life or human sighs!

The cynic laughs awhile but sneers
  Oft hide a bleeding heart of woe!
The snarl is mark of wasted tears,
The lesson what the scornful years
  Have taught a tender heart to know!

'Tis Faith that soonest finds the road
  Which leads to Doubt and Hope's despair;
A Timon bears the greatest load,
Since, trusting all the vicious horde,
  He pays for laying bosom bare!

For throwing bosom bare for ' daws '
  To pluck the heart within their greed;
Voracious here to fill their maws;
Inhuman in observing laws
  Professed to govern Christian creed!

CXXXIII.

In reason then we cry for change
  And hope thereby to find less pain;
Hath not old Nature wider range
Than walks confined which here estrange
  By jostling ill on ill again?

A change! a change! O Heavens, why
  A lagging day, a lazy hour?
A tendium of thought, a sigh
For absent things while those near by
  To satisfy have not the power?

And yet if all things came at will
  Our every wish to gratify,
Would we the happier be? or still
Dissatisfied and deem as ill
  The fortune that attends a sigh?

The unattainable we seek ;
  The thing possessed we oft dispise ;
Regrets and longings make us weak ;
We're constant only to the bleak
  And chill despairs of earthly cries

Unsettled so is life.   Content
  Is something no man ever knew ;
And fruitless are his labors spent
Who thinks by force of his intent
  To gain a measure of his due.

CXXXIV.

The winter hath its moaning winds,
  Its pall and shroud for earth's decay ;
A gloomy dome the eye confinds ;
The Spirit of the year repines
  Within the barren woods and lay.

From leadened skies great flakes come forth
   Like spotless doves from cote on high;
They drift and scatter as though loath
To bide command that sent them forth
   The fleecy troopers of the sky!

They drift and marshal till the earth
   Is covered with a robe of white,
As ermined for some deed of worth,
Or clothed within the shift of dearth
   To hide its barrenness from sight:

And aged seems it then, withal,
   And plaintive, too, its feeble cry;
And mighty trees like spectres tall,
Or monuments of death, recall
   The thoughts to mock of Destiny!

CXXXV.

When hair is colored as the snow,
   And form is bent and eye is dim,
'Tis then man's feebleness we know,
And what repays for all his show
   Of valor battling for life's whim.

He is the sport of Time, withal;
   The play thing of a passing day;
A breath of momentary thrall;
A sigh that flees its own recall;
   An impulse of an atom's play!

His birth is Spark struck from the flint
  Of Unknown Forces, and his youth
And age are rounds of labor's dint
In Nature's workshop; but no hint
  Is given of the natal truth!

Nor of the pause which seasons bring,
  And which we call his earthly death;
The Unknowns to the Unknowns fling
This hyperbolic, flaming, Thing
  We call a Life, a Soul, a Breath!

Man is, and that is all we know:
  He goes, and Speculation's dream
Tells where! No probing here below
Has reached as yet that "Other Shore,"
  However wisely Faith may "deem"!

CXXXVI.

We see our friends around us die;
  We clasp their hands in gripless fold,
And close their eyes, and wonder why
The Beings can so silent lie
  While bodies waste in earthly mould.

The deed is one of love: the thought
  The child of its own mystery.
The Force that moved the one has wrought
Conditions of the other; taught
  The mind its impotence to see!

The earth is parent and the grave
  Of you and me and all we know!
Within its bosom sleep the brave,
And winds sweep through the vaulted nave
  Of Faith, deriding in their blow!

CXXXVII.

Blow, Winds of pitiless death, blow on!
  Blow till your hate in fury dies!
Blow, blow till chilling shades creep on
To drink the rays Hyperion
  Would give the earth to light its skies!

Blow till the Night of Destiny
  Engulfs the cringing soul of Man!
Blow till this mundane sphere is free
Of Life and Love and Phantasy,
  And Death and Hate the ages span!

Blow through the night of Gloom and Ill:
  Blow through the shadowy vale of Death!
Blow till the howl of Manes fill
The echoing cave and barren hill:
  Blow till Destruction gasps for breath!

Blow then on deathless earth your gale—
  Maruts to wake its Life again!
Blow till the buds of Youth regale
The scene once more to blush the pale
  Of Death with blossoms that have been!

Blow! blow Rejuvenescence's dawn!
  Blow life to Hope's perennial Spring!
Blow Youth and Beauty into brawn
Of Manhood with its strength unshorn :
  Blow till the happy welkins ring!

Blow all your bitterness and then
  Blow zephyrs of a soothing fame!
Blow out the fears that once have been ;
Breathe peace and happiness again,
  And fan to life Love's smouldering flame!

www.ingramcontent.com/pod-product-compliance
Lightning Source LLC
Chambersburg PA
CBHW032007010726
47493CB00007B/2302